Wild & Wishful, Dark & Dreaming

The Worlds of
ALETHEA KONTIS

Books of Arilland

Enchanted
Hero
Trixter
Dearest / Messenger
Tales of Arilland
Trix and the Faerie Queen
Thieftess
Trix and the Fire Witch
Fated
Endless
Countenance

Other Titles by Alethea Kontis

Haven, Kansas
Beauty & Dynamite
Wild & Wishful, Dark & Dreaming
Diary of a Mad Scientist Garden Gnome
The Dark-Hunter Companion (w/ Sherrilyn Kenyon)
AlphaOops: The Day Z Went First
AlphaOops: H is for Halloween
The Wonderland Alphabet
Elemental (editor)

Want to know when Alethea has a new book out? Sign up for the newsletter! You'll get brief monthly emails about new releases, book sales, Princess Alethea merchandise, and videos featuring the author princess herself!

Sign up today: http://www.aletheakontis.com

To Ryan, Brenna, Dana, and Andy

For being there

TABLE OF CONTENTS

"Maybe our souls are like the ocean
shouting back colors from the sun
and maybe the sun will hold these answers
when these answers never come."
—Adam Ezra Group, *Another Sunshine*

INTRODUCTION

The first thing I learned about Alethea Kontis (aka the Princess) is that she's a woman of many talents, interests and tiaras. Her interests happen to pattern mine with frightening similarity. It's why we'd been introduced, in a schmoozing-sort of lunch at Book Expo America, organized with the phrase: "I think you'll get along."

The two that brought us together didn't realize they wouldn't get a word in edgewise at lunch. While they went on to other publishing houses and so did we, our well-costumed and tiara bedecked friendship remained; (forever solidified over the ability to move fluidly between a discussion of Star Trek to quoting Steel Magnolias) the sort of "bosom friend" Anne of Green Gables calls Diana.

But just because one becomes instant friends does not guarantee one will champion their friend's work. So I was utterly relieved when I found that my appreciation of Alethea as person and Princess was only magnified by my appreciation of her craft.

What I love about Alethea, from one writer to another, is that I've yet to see a type of storytelling she can't accomplish. She loves nothing more than a challenge. Well, nothing except a *really* good story… She then issues that challenge to herself, her characters, her setting, and always manages to surprise and delight along her labyrinthine paths towards unpredictable endings.

So whether it's fantasy, adventure, children's books, Steampunk, a companion guide to a well-loved series, a love story, a horror story, an alternate history or—my personal favorite—her particular way of reinventing fairy tales, Princess Alethea is always most at home in her realm when she is storytelling. And she invites you, the reader, to share in her realm (she is a very generous Princess).

And so I welcome you to Princess Alethea's many worlds. Make yourself thoroughly at home, for you are in the hands of an elegant, clever and quite magical hostess of Story. I know I'll be enjoying her every kind of Once Upon A Times until the end of my days, and I hope, dear reader, so will you.

—Leanna Renee Hieber

183 Million Light Years from Home

"Captain Yerin," announced Motok, "you asked me to notify you when we were in range. We've registered the beacon on the nearest scout. The signal is strong. We should be receiving the data any minute now."

Yerin moved to stand behind him. "What do you think our chances are, Motok?"

Motok concentrated on his instrument panel. "Hard to say, sir. I'll know more as soon as we have some data."

Yerin grimaced. Motok always said the same thing. He had been saying the same thing for the last hundred and twenty scouts they had recovered. Of course, saying that was probably what had kept Yerin from killing him.

Yerin turned and headed back to his chair, hoping for the hundred and twenty-first time that this was the one.

***

Allen Cooper loosened his tie with his right hand and eased on to I-40 with his left. He turned up the classic rock station and cracked the windows to enjoy the cool, starless summer night. He checked the clock in the dashboard. Sheesh—3 am. He hadn't meant to be starting home this late, but closing the bar down with the head of Tanner Industries was sure to score him major points. There was no sense wasting sixty bucks on a hotel room when Lebanon was only a few hours away. Good tunes, good mood, a couple of beers under the belt, empty roads—well, except for the idiot up ahead with his blinker on—he'd be home well before sunrise.

He got the truck up to 76 and hit the cruise control. He thought about calling Sarah, but she probably wouldn't be able to fully appreciate his enthusiasm at three in the morning. She needed all the sleep she could manage – the morning sickness would hit soon enough as it was. It would have to wait. Oh, that sucked. He was absolutely brimming over with pride and desperately wanted to share it with somebody. He drummed the steering wheel in an enthusiastic solo and let out a hearty cry that would have made Tarzan jealous. I am The Man. Hear me roar.

Brandon Tanner had been excited about the new automated agriculture technology Allen's company had to offer. It had helped that Allen himself was such a fan of the remote crop harvesters and condition monitors. No matter how crazy his family thought he was, come hell or high water, Allen was determined to see farming into the twenty-first century.

Brandon had been the head of Tanner Industries for almost a year now, but he told Allen that he still felt the weight of his old man's shadow, the pressure to be just like a man with whom he had nothing in common. Allen knew all too well what that was like. That same generation gap was what separated him from his own father. So he had commiserated with the young millionaire for many hours over several pitchers of Budweiser. Didn't matter how much money you had. Deep down, every man was a good ol' boy.

Somewhere around 2 am Brandon had decided that what Tanner Industries needed was to grow up, break out of the old way of doing things. New technology was just the way to do it. He told Allen he would have his secretary call Monday and schedule a meeting. The conversation then turned to more pressing matters, like Angelina Jolie's breasts and the fate of the Titans' next season.

It was a good thing Tennessee bars closed so early on Saturdays—he didn't want Brandon so drunk he didn't remember the meeting. That hadn't been the purpose anyway. They had just been two young bucks letting off steam. Good for the soul. Very good for Allen's position. He did hate leaving Sarah alone, though.

She'd be so excited. Allen checked to make sure his phone was on, just in case she caught his psychic messages and tried to get in touch with him. Oh, you have got to be kidding, right? No signal. Piece of junk. He tossed it on the seat beside him. Apparently "nationwide" service meant "nationwide on a clear night in a town with more than one McDonalds."

He leaned forward and scanned the sky. He couldn't see a break in the clouds anywhere. There was a light patch where the moon hid, but nothing else, all the way down to the horizon. And still, less than a mile in front of him, that stupid car had his blinker on. Moron. Did the constant click not drive him nuts? Maybe it was broken. Maybe his radio was up too loud. Maybe the guy just had his hazard lights on, and the back right one was out. But why would he have them on in the first place? No, there was nothing wrong with that car. Except the jerk behind the wheel. Allen flashed his lights a few times. Probably wouldn't do any good.

It didn't.

The radio started to break up. Allen hit the scan button. Nothing came through cleanly, and what did was all about redemption. Whoo-ee. Christians with radio stations that loved to hear themselves talk. Wonder how many people got saved this early in the morning. Just for the heck of it, he tried the AM band. A growling, screeching noise like a car being impacted creamed his eardrums. Quickly, he turned the radio off. He missed his Mazda. He missed his CD player more. Stupid car would have to break down the day before a business trip.

He should have been grateful that Donny had lent him his F-150. Without it, what could possibly turn out to be the greatest night of his life might never have happened. He'd managed it well, seeing Brandon drive off in his Lexus before climbing into the white monster. It would have been too obvious to the world, too obvious that he was the short, brainiac son in a family of gargantuan, truck-driving farmers. Men in suits and ties who were less than six feet tall did not drive crew cabs.

And if they did, they'd have at least had a CD player installed.

Blink. Blink. Blink. Blink.

He was more tired than he thought.

Allen reached for his jacket, fumbling for the pocket. Aw, man. One cigarette left. Had they really smoked the whole pack? Sarah would kill him if she found that out. Well, so, she wouldn't find out. But it certainly didn't help his effort to stop before the baby came.

The baby.

Well, that train of thought should keep him up for a while. Allen lit the smoke and rolled the window down all the way. The baby had been Sarah's little surprise before he'd left.

"You don't seem happy about it."

"Happy? I am happy. Thrilled. I'd be more thrilled if I wasn't so worried about this Tanner thing."

"It's Saturday," she said. "Why do you have to go on a Saturday?"

"'Cause you go when the executives pencil you in, Sarah."

"Well, I'd love if you could pencil me in sometime." She turned away from him, and Allen heard her breath catch. He rolled his eyes. It was an old argument. And he knew just how it ended.

"That's it, baby," he said. "Forget the meeting. Come here." He grabbed the tie of her robe and pulled her into his arms. She shrieked. They fell back onto the rumpled sheets, and he kissed her neck until she squealed. "Oh, God." He pulled away from her. "I didn't hurt anything, did I?" He let his hand drift down to her stomach.

"No," her eyes were a little shiny. "You didn't. For once."

"I'm happy, Sarah, really," Allen said. "And I'm going to go to work, and I'm gonna give this Tanner guy all I've got, and I'm going to get that promotion that Fitzgerald keeps dangling in front of my face. And we'll finally have enough. And it will all work. Okay?" She nodded, her brows crinkling as she fought off tears. He kissed her forehead. "You look so beautiful when there's snot dripping out of your nose."

"Rat." She punched him in the shoulder.

Thudthudthudthudthud—

Allen snapped to attention and swerved left, off the grooves of the emergency lane. The cigarette. Oh, crap. He smacked all over his clothes, shifting as far as he could in his seat without taking his hand off the wheel. There — floorboard. He flicked it out the window with a sigh. So much for that distraction.

It was all blinker guy's fault. The constant yellow flash was like a swinging pendulum. It was hypnotizing him to death. He looked over at the dashboard. He hadn't even been on the road an hour yet. Fantastic. He needed a new distraction.

He tried the radio again, turning the volume all the way down in case he caught that feedback noise again. At first he heard nothing, so he turned it up louder. There was a soft, steady series of beeps, like a heart monitor. He hit scan. The readout ran through the entire AM band until it came back to the beeps. He switched to FM. Nothing but static. Well, that was a lost cause. Even the Christians would have provided him with some amusement.

He caught another blinking light out of the corner of his eye, this one white. A mobile phone tower. It was up ahead, on his right. Good. He'd call Fitzgerald's office and leave a long message on his answering machine. He'd call Sarah and wake her up anyway. She'd sacrifice a good night's sleep to keep the father of her child awake, wouldn't she?

Blink. Blink. Blink.

He grabbed the cell phone. Battery, yes. Service, no. What?? He aimed the phone at the blinking light of the tower as he passed by. "HELLO! I'M RIGHT HERE!"

Nothing.

"That's it. I'm canceling my service." He threw the phone back onto the seat. He rolled down all the other windows. He tried singing at the top of his lungs, but the only thing that came to mind was "John Jacob Jingleheimerschmidt," and that got old after a few rounds. Just for fun, he turned his left blinker on and left it on. He flicked off the cruise control and sped up. He was going to pass this guy and give him a taste of his own medicine.

Was it a guy, or a chick? A chick driving an SUV? He couldn't tell. Looked like a guy. A big guy. A really big guy with huge Bob Marley dreadlocks. Allen was about three car-lengths behind when he realized he was going 95. He lifted his foot off the accelerator. Blinker guy slowed down too.

"Oh, now come on," he muttered. Allen flashed his lights at the guy again.

Nothing.

He moved over one lane to the right. Blinker guy moved over too. Allen moved back to the left. The SUV swerved in front of him.

Oh, so that was his game, was it?

Allen turned his own blinker off. It may not have been making the guy up ahead nuts, but the metallic, repetitive noise was driving him insane. He laid on his horn. Nothing.

All right, the guy didn't intend to let him pass. He could pull off onto an exit, wait a while and then come back on, but he didn't want to. He wanted to get home, to his nice warm bed and his nice warm wife. He wasn't going to let this guy get away with owning the road just because he was an idiot. He tried to pass again, but the SUV would not let him.

Blink. Blink.

Fine. He'd tough it out. Allen slowed, putting some space between them.

Allen blinked his eyes a couple of times. He turned on the air conditioner full blast. He tried the radio again. No beeps this time, but a strange string of seemingly unpronounceable words. Great. Now the Christians were speaking in tongues. He turned it back off. He banged his head on the steering wheel. He tried to burp the alphabet forwards, and then backwards. It took him three tries to do it with no mistakes.

He had only wasted ten more minutes.

Two hours to go.

"AAAAAAAAAAARGH!" He yelled at the top of his lungs.

It didn't help.

Nothing helped.

If only he hadn't gone through all his smokes. That would have at least given him something to do with his hands. There was no sense looking around in the truck for any, Donny didn't smoke. Oh, wait. But some of his employees did. Maybe he'd get lucky.

Allen stretched out and popped the glove compartment open. Well, lookie what we have here. The coyote gun. He'd forgotten all about it.

Much better than cigarettes.

Nobody suffered coyotes in Tennessee, especially men who owned cattle. Donny had taken him on a coyote hunt right before Allen had left for college. Those guys may have been rednecks, but they would have made some pretty good marines. Donny had sped across the pasture in this very same truck.

"Lean back." That was all Donny had said. And he had fired the pistol right in front of Allen's face.

Allen, deaf from the shot and shocked by the suddenness of it, had the piece of mind to turn his head to the right and watch a coyote drop like a rock. Donny had just smiled. Allen had had to buy the beer that night.

He shook the pistol gently in his hand, feeling its weight. It had been a while since he'd shot cans off the back fence, but his aim had always been good. Just another one of the reasons his father thought college a waste of a good man. He checked the clip. Yup. He only needed one bullet. If that guy's blinker wasn't broken before, it would be now.

***

"The transmissions we're receiving from the scout look good, Captain Yerin. So far, this looks like a viable planet."

The captain stood, tossing his tentacles back from his face. "Excellent. Prepare the exterminant, and fire on my mark."

"Captain? The transmission isn't finished uploading."

"Motok, the sooner we can rid this place of vermin, the sooner we can send for the agrobiologists and get out of here. If there's anything wrong with this place, it'll be their problem. Fire on my mark. Three-two-one—"

***

Allen's foot hit the gas. The truck sprang forward, gaining. 90. 95. Almost 100. Close enough. He feinted to the left, swerved to the right and fired out his window.

He missed the blinker.

He hit the tire.

The guy fishtailed ahead of him, and then flew off the road into the ditch to the right.

"Ha! Shows you, jerk!" Allen sped off, into the night.

He was still holding the gun. He put the safety back on and set it on the seat. Still chuckling, he looked in the rear view mirror.

There was a flash. Orange this time. Red. A bigger flash. The car was on fire. Had that been the pop of the gas tank exploding, or had he just imagined it?

"Oh my God."

***

"Captain, we've lost the signal!" Motok spun around in his chair, blinking all four eyes in disbelief.

"You've got to be kidding." Captain Yerin stalked over to Motok's position. A slime trail followed him across the slick floor.

"No, sir." said Motok. "It must have been discovered."

"Nonsense. I've seen these scouts camouflage themselves. They're absolutely undetectable; none of our scanning equipment has ever picked one up once it's integrated itself. I can't believe the life on this planet has such intelligence. Has it gone underground?"

"No, sir, it would have left some sort of trace. We would only have complete loss of signal if the scout were destroyed. Either something on the planet did it, or the scout risked discovery and self-terminated."

***

Allen took his foot off the gas. He was still pushing 100. He couldn't risk being pulled over by the cops. He brought it down to 65.

What had he done?

He couldn't turn around. He shouldn't. There was nothing he could do for the guy now. He would only be questioned by the authorities, once they found the wreck. He checked his phone again. Still no signal. He couldn't even call it in. The cops would have to find the guy in their own good time. By then, Allen would be safely past Nashville.

Cops had CBs, though. They could put up a roadblock. He had to get rid of that gun. He watched enough television to know how it would go down. They would discover the bullet imbedded in the tire, and they'd find the match. Wait. He hadn't passed the river yet, had he? Allen sweated every minute until he got to the bridge and pulled over. He wiped every inch of the gun off on his shirt, wound up, and pitched it as far as he could. He couldn't even hear the splash as it went in.

He leaned his head back against the truck. What on earth had possessed him? It must have been the beer. Maybe he had had more to drink than he thought. No, it was the lack of sleep. Or the meeting. Or all three. Yeah. Beer and lack of sleep, and the giddiness over the successful meeting.

No.

It had been him.

The brain he had respected for so long, the one thing that had set him apart from his family, had betrayed him. He'd just bought himself a one-way ticket to hell. You could take the boy out of the country, but you couldn't take the country out of the boy. A man like him didn't deserve to have a child. He looked down into the dark, churning waters of the river. Maybe that was the solution. Maybe that was the only way out. Maybe that was all he deserved.

***

The captain leaned his head back and let out a long roar that made several officers pass out. He saw them hit the floor and lowered his anger to a growl. "Wasted," he snarled. "All this time wasted on the only harvestable planet in this galaxy. What were they thinking, sending us to answer a beacon all the way out here?"

"What should we do, sir? Should we send out another scout, just to be sure?"

"No. The agrobiologists will discount any planet where a scout has been destroyed." Yerin turned and slowly made his way back to his chair. He sat. The cabin was silent. "We have no choice but to abort."

"Are you sure, Captain?" asked Motok.

Yerin curled a lip, rows of teeth flashing in the light of his console. "They wanted to make a fool out of me, and they have. I will not pursue this matter further. Maneuver us into position for lightjump. Take us Home."

"Yes, Captain." Motok turned back to his control board and punched in the coordinates.

***

The phone rang, and Allen jumped. Heart racing, he reached through the window and snatched it off the seat.

"Hello?"

"Allen? Sweetie? What's wrong?"

"What? Sarah. Oh, nothing. Nothing's wrong. I'm fine. I mean, I'm tired. Just tired. I had to pull over for a minute."

"Allen, honey, stay somewhere if you need to."

"No, no, I'm fine, really. There's nothing out here anyway. I just want to be home with you. Oh, my God, what time is it? Are you okay?"

She laughed. "Well, I thought I was having a heart attack; apparently, it's just heartburn. I'm sure I'll be paying homage to the porcelain God once you get home, though, and things will be right back to normal. Did your meeting go well? I've been dying to know."

This was why he loved Sarah. Everything in Sarah's world was sunshiny and full of life. "It went…fantastic, actually."

"Well, don't keep me in suspense, silly! Tell me everything! Help me keep my mind off my bodily functions."

"Yeah. Look, let me call you back when I'm on the road, okay?"

"Okay."

"And Sarah?"

"Yeah?"

He took a deep breath. "I love you."

"I love you, too, you fool. Be careful."

"I will."

Allen ended the call and looked up at the sky. The clouds were breaking, and the stars began to wink through. He closed his eyes. Please, he wished. Please let this all go away. Please let me get on with my life. Give me a second chance. I'll do my best; I'll make it all right. I'll give Sarah everything she needs. I'll teach my son to be a better man than his father.

Please.

Allen wiped the tears from his eyes as he watched a star shoot across the sky and then disappear.

Blink.

The heavens had answered.

BLOOD, SWEAT, AND TEARS

Angelica Monroe was a Diva. "Angelica Monroe" wasn't even her real name; it was Lois. She was the ninth of twelve children born to a poor farmer and his wife—Mr. and Mrs. Daniel Lane—in backwoods North Carolina. Lois had married young and gotten pregnant, not necessarily in that order. She raised her sickly child in a vermin-infested death trap, lied on loans to put her husband through medical school, skipped meals to keep her family fed. In a last desperate effort to stay sane, she started writing novels. She submitted manuscripts under the name Angelica Monroe, a nom de plume invented in honor of her two heroines Angelica Houston and Marilyn Monroe. (She was sure no one would publish anything written by Lois Lane.) On the very last day, the day the landlord posted the eviction notice, the day she had to walk baby Zachary to the ER in the pouring rain, the day she gave up writing…she got the phone call. A publisher wanted to buy her novel. In less than five short years, Angelica Monroe had clawed herself up from that leaky basement apartment to the top of the *New York Times* bestseller list.

Anyone who asked Angelica the secret to her success got the

same answer, accompanied by the same sly grin. "Blood, sweat, and tears, sweetie pie. Blood, sweat, and tears." That's the story she told, and that's the story everyone fell in love with. And it was the truth. Sort of.

Angelica could have given Madonna a run for her money in the Reinventing Your Image department. She wrote different books under different names for different publishers in different genres. Everything she touched turned to gold. She could do no wrong. Angelica Monroe was a charmed woman. Then her beloved husband of over twenty years died suddenly and unexpectedly, and Angelica's world died with him. Her son was shipped off to boarding school abroad. Angelica went on sabbatical, hiding out in a cabin in an undisclosed location in the Blue Ridge Mountains.

There were no more books released. None.

Fans of Angelica Monroe all over the world yearned, suffered, and mourned with her. The publishing industry suffered as well. Publishers re-released Angelica with new art, in boxed-sets, omnibuses, and limited-edition leatherbound hardcovers. But it was no substitute for the real thing.

Twenty-eight months later, the buzz started. Wild rumors circulated: Angelica Monroe was back from seclusion with an all new series. It was haunting and cathartic and something—yet again—entirely different. The marketing budget could have fed a small country. Talk show requests flooded the interwebs. Independent bookstore owners crossed their fingers and prayed that people would start reading again. Offset printers backlogged all their customers and jockeyed for position.

Three years to the day of her husband's death, Angelica Monroe magically appeared on the streets of New York, dressed to the nines for the launch of her new paranormal romance, *The Gypsy*. Once again everything was right with the world, and six billion people breathed a collective sigh of relief. Not surprisingly, the book debuted at number one on all the lists and stayed there, week after week.

When people asked Angelica how she did it, her answer was the same as it had been all those years ago. "Blood, sweat, and tears, sweetie pie. Blood, sweat, and tears."

***

Desi balanced the lunch tray in both hands and tried not to trip up the stairs. A Coke and a Weight Watchers bar probably didn't warrant this much ceremony, but she thought Angelica might appreciate it. Desi would have appreciated it if someone brought her lunch and a coloring book and Gerber daisies when she was sick. Big, bright Crayolas and Gerber daisies always made her smile.

Angelica wouldn't remember it, but there had been Gerber daisies on the table in the Ashville bookstore where they'd met. For some strange reason there had been little else: no banner, no flyer in the window, no announcement in the store that a *New York Times* bestselling author was signing her new book. Angelica had weathered it beautifully. Out of pity, Desi had bought three books and talked to her for an hour and a half. Angelica had been delightful and sweet, and she had seemed genuinely interested in Desi's gypsy family heritage, a heritage as white-trash at its heart as her own. As Desi walked back to her car that day she felt a little sad; fame and fortune aside, Angelica Monroe would have been a really great girlfriend to hang out with. The butterflies in her stomach told her to stop hoping for the impossible. Three days later there was an email from Angelica in her inbox.

Desi gently knocked three times.

"Come in."

Desi eased the door open with her foot and maneuvered the tray inside the bedroom.

"Oh, sweetie," Angelica said in a strained, scratchy voice, "you didn't have to do all that." She lay on the bed with all the grace of a fallen movie star tucked under her white down comforter, platinum blonde hair carelessly strewn behind her on the pillowcase. Angelica's hair had been titian when they had met that fateful day in the bookstore. It had later transformed into mahogany, then black, and now blonde, with streaks of violet and fire engine red thrown in for good measure.

"I know." Desi set the tray down on top of the mini fridge that doubled as a bedside table and settled herself on the edge of the bed. "I thought it might make you smile."

"Smiling is"—Angelica's body shook with a series of painfully raspy coughs—"the only thing that doesn't hurt." Desi unscrewed the cap on the Coke bottle and waited while Angelica took a few sips. Angelica handed it back and sunk into her pillow with a grin.

"See? There's my reward," said Desi. "I'd do anything for that smile."

"Want to write a book for me?" It was a stock question. Angelica was always on deadline for one thing or another. Between all the publishers and all the series, the only way Desi ever got to see

Angelica was when she showed up on the doorstep of her cabin and physically dragged her away from the computer.

"You know I would if I could." It was Desi's standard reply.

"It's not that hard."

Desi unwrapped the meal replacement bar. "Honey, I could sit down and I could write the words, but it would never sound like you. Not in a million years."

Angelica didn't move to take the food. She looked Desi straight in the eyes. "You could." She was serious.

Desi raised an eyebrow. This was a turn the conversation had never taken before. "How?"

Angelica smiled again, a sister-in-crime. "I've wanted to show you this for a long time. If"—Desi handed the Coke back to her and waited for the coughing to pass—"I knew if anybody could understand, it would be you. But you have to promise not to tell anyone."

"I promise."

"You have to *swear*, Desi."

Desi whispered a gypsy word of power and traced a quick symbol in the air with her finger. The eddies glowed briefly, and then vanished. "I promise," she repeated.

Giddy, Angelica leaned down and opened the mini fridge. She popped open a section that Desi had assumed until now was for ice trays. Instead it held clear bags full of...blood?

Angelica placed one of the small, heavy plastic bags in her hands. Yes, it was definitely blood. More than blood. Desi knew without having to ask. She was holding the oft proclaimed secret to Angelica Monroe's success: blood, sweat, and tears. It was a simple enough potion, passed down through the ages that had eventually turned it into colloquial slang.

Desi was dumbstruck.

Not that Angelica dabbling in old school magic was much of a surprise; Angelica had an obsession with all of the old magicks and the paranoia to go along with it. Every day was Halloween with Angelica. She saved candles, even after the wicks had burnt down to nothing. She never clipped her finger- or toenails in a public place; she never cleaned out her hairbrush in a hotel room. She had a closet full of Gothic costumes and wigs as her everyday wear. She changed her image every few months to hide from the evil spirits that might be using her likeness to track her down and curse her. Desi, having grown up in a household where superstitions were sewn in the quilts and sown in the garden soil, wrote Angelica's quirks off as…well…quirks.

The fact that Desi was right now holding a bag of Angelica's blood didn't phase her. What boggled her mind was the fact that at some point, to properly complete the spell, Angelica Monroe had actually cried.

"I write with it," Angelica whispered.

"That much I figured."

"I don't write the whole thing out, of course," she went on. "That would take too long. I only do the first few pages, and the last few pages, and"—the coughs racked her again—"some of the pages in between if I get stuck." She gasped and sipped some more soda.

"Except *The Gypsy*," Desi guessed.

"Yes." Angelica closed her eyes. "*The Gypsy* I did longhand. Every page."

Desi tried to imagine the size and the scope of undertaking a manuscript entirely written in blood, sweat, tears…and obviously some sort of anti-coagulant, but such a thing wouldn't have been difficult to obtain for someone as driven as Angelica Monroe. That explained the lengthy hiatus. It explained why *The Gypsy* had debuted at the top of every chart. It explained the adoring fans, the compulsive readers. Angelica had stacked the deck of the New York publishing game and wrapped them around her little finger with a spell that had been around longer than Christianity.

Desi couldn't stop the laugh that burst out of her. She handed the blood back to Angelica and shook her head.

Angelica made no move take it from her. "Will you do it for me?"

Desi sobered.

"My deadline's in a month. If I'm late again, this publisher will have my head. Even if you just write the first few—"

"Yes."

Angelica started at Desi's sudden reply. "You will?"

"I will."

"Oh, sweetie, you're a star!" Angelica croaked. She leapt from under the duvet and wrapped Desi in her arms. "Here, we'll make it official." She slid the coloring book from the tray Desi had brought and ripped off the back cover. She pulled a forest green crayon from the box. "What should we call the book?"

Desi shrugged. "Does it matter? The publisher's just going to rename it anyway."

"But what are *we* going to call it? Just between us. Any title you want."

Desi knew what she would have called the sequel three seconds after she had finished the first book. "*Gypsy Child*."

"Perfect." In a neat, round hand—round being the only option for neat with a green Crayola—Angelica wrote out a basic contract. Desi would get half of the advance and half of the royalties for her work on *Gypsy Child*. Desi read upside-down as she wrote and nodded when Angelica was finished. Angelica drew two lines at the bottom for their signatures.

"Looks good to me," she agreed. Desi reached for the royal purple.

"No," said Angelica. "We have to do this right." She rolled to the other bedside table and rummaged through the clutter there until she found a rogue straight pin and a lighter. "Here."

She pricked her index finger with the pin and squeezed a drop of blood on the paper. She used the pin to scratch her name in blood across the line. It took three drops to get her whole name in. She wiped the pin off with the hem of her shirt, held it in the flame of the lighter until the end turned bright red, wiped it off again, and gave it to Desi. "Your turn, sweetie."

Desi ignored the tug in the pit of her stomach that her Noni would have slapped her for ignoring in days past. She stuck her finger and smeared the blood onto the paper. *Despina Romany*. The letters glowed for a brief second, like the sigil she had drawn in the air, and then dimmed. The butterflies in her stomach remained. Desi wondered if this was what every author felt like when she sold her soul for a five percent royalty.

Angelica touched her cheek reassuringly. "It's going to be a bestseller."

Those butterflies kept Desi company the first time she sat down at Angelica's desk, the desk with the window overlooking the pond with the ducks and the willow tree, the desk that held a fresh ream of paper and an inkpot full of Angelica's blood. Desi had never really used a fountain pen before; the blood dried up faster than she could get it down on paper.

The first page was a slaughter. Desi had to clean the pen out every fifteen minutes. She had blood on her hands and her face, on her clothes and in her hair. It stained the desktop, the blotter, and the thousands of paper towels that only made things a million times worse.

Eventually, though, she got the hang of it. She discovered the angle at which to hold the pen so that it wouldn't smear so much. She worked out how much blood she should put in the pen at a time: enough to keep her writing at a steady pace, but not so much that it dried up and forced her to keep cleaning out the pen.

Desi wrote and wrote and the words were hers, disguised under the clever glamour of Angelica Monroe. Every sentence that came out of her amazed her. The characters became her family; they made her laugh and cry. The story was her world, and she lived comfortably inside it. By the time Angelica recuperated, Desi was half done with the book and showed no sign of stopping. She fell in love with being a writer. She finally understood the escape, the obsession, the pain.

When Desi wrote the last word on the last page, she wept, for she had never before suffered so much in her life, and she never wanted anything as much as she wanted to do it all over again.

Angelica did not dissuade her. She continued going about the business of being the author on parade: dressing up for conventions, making appearances at workshops, giving speeches to standing-room only audiences, and accepting awards at banquets all over the world. She did tours and signed books and kissed cheeks and hugged babies and everyone loved her. They loved her ever-changing persona and the never-changing dark costumes.

Desi made the deadlines. Every single one. And they were all bestsellers. Every single one.

In Desi's eyes, she had the perfect life. She could be the author and create without interruption while Angelica played the face of the woman everyone adored. For every book Desi wrote, she and Angelica made up a separate contract in green crayon and signed it in blood. It never bothered Desi. She wanted for nothing: she had no bills, no day job, no worries. Anything she desired, Angelica provided.

She made a pretty nest egg for herself off the money Angelica gave her for writing, but she never touched it. That was her future, a future she didn't want to think about apart from the knowledge that she wouldn't have to worry when it arrived. For the moment, this perfect moment, she let Angelica use her, and bleed for her, and leave her to her gypsy world behind the desk and the pond with the ducks and the willow tree.

Desi was happy. Her life was complete. Had everything stayed the same, she could have lived that way forever. But nothing ever stays the same. Her Noni taught her that too.

Based on history, Desi shouldn't have been surprised when Angelica's paranoia reared its ugly head. Everyone is afraid of something, something specific, something personal, something they fear worse than death. Angelica Monroe was afraid that she would lose it all, this storybook life she had made for herself and all the material things that filled it. She would lose it all and be tossed back into the nothing from whence she came. Even worse, she was convinced that she wouldn't just lose it—someone would take it from her. Someone like Desi. It was only a matter of time.

Desi noticed when the phone stopped ringing. Angelica had a habit of calling her from one soiree or another to tell her all the stories of what she won, where she ate dinner, who she'd met…and whom she'd left the party with. Like a horny prom date, the phone calls were the first to go. The long, elaborate, conversational emails became briefer and less frequent, until they were subject-line-only telegrams sent through cyberspace to answer direct questions. Angelica stayed gone for days at a time, and then weeks. On the days she was home, they barely spoke to one another.

If Angelica had said anything, at any time, Desi would have stopped writing the books. But she didn't, so Desi kept going. She thought it was what Angelica wanted. She thought that maybe if she waited long enough, Angelica would move on to the next obsession and she and Desi could go back to being the friends they were before. Time, Desi told herself. Just give her time. And she dipped the pen in the bloodpot and wrote on.

When the phone finally did ring, it scared the life out of her. Desi took off her headphones and pressed the button on the receiver. "Hello?"

"Desi? It's Zack. Where's my mom?"

"What's wrong?" Desi paused the music she could still hear

blaring through the earbuds.

"It doesn't matter. I need Mom. Do you know where she is?"

"She's…um…" Desi looked around frantically for a calendar. The whiteboards that normally held Angelica's schedule had stopped being updated three months ago. She knocked the computer awake and moused over the timestamp in the toolbar. October twenty-fourth. What was October…? Oh, right. "She's at the Romance Writers Masquerade this weekend."

"Where the hell is that?" He sounded frantic.

"Atlanta. Hold on, let me Google the hotel." Desi tried to hurry. She could hear Zack's labored breathing over the phone. Were those sirens in the background? "The Hilton. It's being held at the Downtown Hilton. Zack, sweetie, are you—"

"Don't call me that." The line went dead. Okay or not, Zack was gone.

Desi tried to go back to the manuscript, but she couldn't concentrate. She was worried about Zack. If he was in as much trouble as it sounded like, then Desi was worried about Angelica too. Most of all, she was bothered by the fact that she had no idea what was going on. Her best friend had become a complete stranger.

She laid the pen down, pushed her chair back from the desk, and stood up. It was dark outside, the crescent moon barely illuminating the ripples of the pond and the bare limbs of the willow tree. It was darker inside, the only light in the cabin was the lamp on the desk. So dark, and so quiet. So incredibly alone.

Had it always been like this? And for how long? Desi had hardly come up for air long enough to remember. What had it been like for Angelica those two years in the dark and the quiet? Had she even noticed? Or had it made her just the tiniest bit… Well, no wonder she loved all the social events so much. Desi couldn't begrudge her that.

Desi walked up the stairs in the dark and the shadows, like a ghost haunting someone else's life. She wasn't quite sure why she didn't turn on any lights. Perhaps the butterflies knew that secrets fled from the light just like any other intruder. Shadow was their natural habitat. They would be easier to find if she was on common ground.

Desi wanted to get to know her friend again, secrets and all. She pushed open the door to Angelica's room. The raw silk curtains waved in the almost-moonlight that caught in the charms on her bracelet. The duvet was now black lace, with a red ribbon woven at its edge. Desi made her way to the mini fridge and opened it. The neverending bottles of Coke stared back at her. She slid open the panel to look at the small bags that waited for her, the bags filled with Angelica's blood, sweat, and tears. Desi wondered again what Angelica had to cry about. Maybe she collected tears by plucking her nostril hairs, or sniffing hot pepper—the tricks most actresses used.

Desi walked around to the other side of the bed and perched on the edge. She smoothed the red satin pillowcase with her hand and wished her glass half-full again. There was a pad of paper there on the table by the phone, with numbers scribbled on it in a neat, round hand. The green crayon was worn down to the nub.

When a tear fell from her cheek, Desi's first thought was that she should probably collect it. She pushed it out of her mind. That crayon was proof; she had to believe it. Somewhere, deep down, the same old Angelica still loved her, the same old Angelica that went to movies with her and vented about other authors over Starbucks. Their friendship could survive, if Desi could just find a way to get through to her.

Desi sniffled, and then laughed. While tears could be useful, snot was part of no spell that could help her in this situation. She scanned the bedroom for a tissue. Angelica always had a box of tissues around for no reason; it was a habit Angelica got from her vapor-happy mother. Desi yanked open the drawer in the nightstand and lost her train of thought completely when she saw the doll.

It was a miniature in candlewax, its head obscured by a translucent red fabric. Tulle, maybe, or chiffon. Not that it mattered. The spell was the same. Love. Obsession. Addiction. Blindness. The doll wore a soft cotton shirt and a long, patchwork skirt that mirrored the ones Desi was so fond of. She didn't need to unwrap the doll to know whose long brown hair was stuck in the wax, whose likeness would stare back at her. She unwrapped the doll to see, to undo its spell. The butterflies in her stomach cheered in triumph.

Desi drew a symbol in the air and whispered the word for cleansing. The air and the doll glowed brightly, scaring the shadows away in shame. When the light dimmed, Desi could see, clearer than she had ever seen before. Cobwebs in the corners. A stain on the pillowcase. Dust riding the beams of pale moonlight that slanted in the window. Herself in the mirror, a tired, dark-eyed shadow of who she once was. When had she last bathed? When had she last eaten? She looked like a prisoner in her own skin.

Silently, Desi shut the drawer. She stood, smoothed the duvet, and put the doll in her skirt pocket. She did not stop to wash her face. She did not stop to eat, despite her growling stomach. Desi walked back down the stairs and settled herself into the chair behind the desk. After a minute of staring out into the chilly October night, she dipped the pen in the bloodpot and started writing again.

***

Angelica came home a week later. Desi had remained at the cabin, just in case Zack called again. Just in case Angelica had needed her. Just in case Angelica remembered she existed.

Desi turned the light on when she heard the keys scratching against the lock, and she opened the door. Angelica looked like hell. Her eyes were bloodshot and her hair—in a Betty Paige-do, long and dark with severe bangs—was wild, like she'd been driving her little red Mustang breakneck along the windy mountain roads with the top down. "Are you okay?"

"Fine." Angelica fumbled with her suitcases and pushed her way in.

"Did Zack get in touch with you? Is everything okay?"

Angelica kicked the heavy, costume-laden suitcases across the floor. "It's none of your business."

"Of course it's my business." Desi grabbed Angelica's hand before she could escape up the stairs. "I'm your friend."

Angelica yanked her arm away. "Sweetie pie, you are my *employee*," she spat. She tried to heft both the suitcases up the stairs at once, but she gave up. She could only lift one. Desi sighed and let Angelica awkwardly tromp up the stairs and slam the door to her room. After a minute, she followed with the other case.

She set it on the landing and knocked on the door. "Angelica, can I—"

The door swung open. Angelica stared back at Desi with her red, accusing eyes, the bright light encircling her riotous mop of hair in a golden a halo. "You found the doll."

Oh, blast the stupid doll. "I don't care about the doll, Angelica. I care about you. Will you please tell me what's going on?"

Apparently, whatever drugs or drink or adrenaline Angelica was on had stopped up her ears. "You found the doll and now you want to kill me."

"Angelica, what the hell are you talking about?"

"I know," she rambled on. "You want retribution. You always have. You've been stewing down there, working away, under my spell. Now that you know it was me who did this to you, you want payback. Don't lie to me. I know."

Desi slapped her, much like any sane woman would have slapped a hysterical friend. "You know nothing, because you don't talk to me anymore."

"I don't have to. I know what you want. You want to get back at me for what I did. Well, let me tell you right now, it will do you no good. If I die, nothing goes to you. Do you hear me? I've willed it all to Zack. You get nothing."

Desi grabbed Angelica by the arms. "I. Don't. Want. It," she said evenly. "I don't want any of it. I never did. All this stuff you have, the life you live—it's not mine, and I don't want it to be."

Desi shook Angelica, forcing her to concentrate. "I only ever wanted to be your friend. I care about you, Angelica. I cared about you before you cast your silly little spell, which is why it made little difference. You would know that if you ever talked to me, if you ever trusted me."

"I can't trust anyone," she whispered. "Especially not you. You're just like my husband."

Desi winced. She didn't want to know what had happened to Angelica's husband, but it made sense. Angelica would have tested the dolls at some point, to know that they even worked. She had probably even magicked herself ill when she had conned Desi into writing the first book for her.

But Angelica wasn't listening. There was no use doing a spell to make something happen that already existed. She'd been wishing for something she already had. The feelings were already there; a spell wasn't going to make them any different. Desi had loved both books and Angelica long before any of this, and that had never changed.

But there would be no changing Angelica's mind in this state. The paranoia inside kept her ranting, kept her inventing preposterous lies. It was far easier for Angelica to believe those lies than it was for her to trust someone. It was then that Desi realized: Angelica Monroe's worst fear was Angelica Monroe. If she continued down this path, she would soon destroy herself and everything around her. And everyone who loved her. Desi. Zack. The fans. The publishers. Everyone.

Desi reached out for Angelica again and missed. The charms of her bracelet caught in Angelica's untamed hair, and Angelica tore herself away. "Stop pretending to be my friend!" she screamed. "You know nothing about me. Just go away!"

Desi stood her ground. "Angelica, you're not making any sense. I am not leaving here until you calm down and we discuss this like rational people."

"Fine. If you're not leaving, then I will." She snatched up her purse and stormed out, the hounds of hell all but baying in her wake. The door slammed, Louboutin heels clacked on Spanish paving stones, and the wheels of the Mustang screeched out of the driveway.

Desi let out a long breath. Her shoulders sank, and her heart with them. She flipped the light switch off and let the shadows of the night comfort her in her sadness.

She pulled the candlewax doll from her skirt pocket. She had cleansed it, wiped it of any trace of her likeness. It was warm from her body heat. She pulled the fine, dark hairs still trapped in the links of her bracelet and pressed them into the head of the doll. It was Halloween. It wouldn't take the spirits long to find Angelica on this night of all nights, when they were strongest and could smell fear.

Angelica would have reached the windy roads by now, the part of the mountains she loved this time of year, where the bright moon kissed the rainbow of golden-red leaves that decorated the valley. Autumn's brilliant Technicolor finale before the quiet, beautiful white death of winter.

Desi got a tissue from the bathroom and wiped her tears with it. Then she folded the tissue up into a long, thin strip and wrapped it around the doll's head. But instead of blinding the doll as

Angelica had blinded her, Desi wished for Angelica to *see*. Angelica would see herself and how she wove into the tapestry of the world. She would see her actions, and how they affected everyone. She would see exactly how much she had what everyone else coveted: beauty, talent, money, fame, power. How Angelica Monroe decided to live her fabulous life beyond that point would be her choice.

Desi put the doll back into her pocket and resumed her writing. There was nothing more she could do.

***

Angelica Monroe died on Halloween night in a blaze of fire and steel. So beautiful and so young. Too young. It was all very epic and glamorous.

Once again, the world mourned. The publishers instantly sold out of all her books. Nothing like a little death to boost sales. Overnight, Zachary Monroe had enough money to bail himself out of any jail in the world for the rest of his tormented life.

Desi was approached at the funeral by three publishers asking if she would write a biography-slash-memoir of the time she'd spent with Angelica and their close friendship. Six days later, her contract went to the highest bidder. She signed it with a blue ballpoint and faxed it back to her agent. The butterflies didn't even notice.

Desi left the cabin to sit behind a new desk in a new apartment. The window beyond it looked down onto a street full of children, laughing and screaming as they chased each other in the dusk, forcing all the energy they could into those last fleeting moments before the streetlamps called them in for supper.

With a deep breath, she opened the thick notebook in front of her to the first clean page. If she never started this, she would never finish. Desi reached for her pen, and the band-aid in the crook of her elbow pulled painfully at the hairs on her arm. At least she knew what the title would be. That was always a good place to start.

Blood, Sweat, and Tears, she wrote, *by Despina Romany*. Now. Where to begin. *Angelica Monroe was a Diva*. No, no…that was a little too close to the truth. She needed something a little…softer around the edges.

Angelica Monroe was a Goddess, and I will miss her generous heart. There. And it was even the truth. Sort of.

Inspired, Desi dipped her pen in the bloodpot and wrote on. It was going to be a bestseller.

FOILED

To kakosu, to kero.

The day she had asked her father what the words meant, he had slapped her. She had overheard the Aunts, she admitted. He went very still after that, and simply told her to never say them again. The words were a curse: *May each day you live after this be worse than the one before.*

She had known better than to say the words. She had known better…but it hadn't stopped her. It was in her blood, the Aunts said. The blood of the Old World. It was the only part of her she couldn't run away from. Blood cannot become water, they said.

Knock, knock, knock.

"Come on, Allie. I know you're in there."

She had tried for thirty years to be the perfect child. She had always been gentle and kind and generous. She had done her best to put goodness out into the world, so that goodness always came back to her. The Aunts said her soul shone like a rainbow. Animals ate from her hand. Children flocked to her wherever she went.

And men had used her like a doormat. This last one had been the worst. She had to draw a line somewhere. She had to stand her ground. She had to believe in herself, or no one else would.

"You have to help me, Allie," he called from the porch. "I can't live like this."

As if that was justification. She had spent four years of her life taking care of him, providing for him, encouraging him, waiting for him to live up to his potential. Only he was quite content in his life of mediocrity…quite content to let Allie take care of him forever. A year and a half after breaking it off, she was still cleaning up his messes. How was that fair?

"Alllllllll-ieeeeee." It was a desperate moan.

He deserved everything he got. After all he had put her through, he deserved some hell of his own. A year and a half ago. It had taken him that long to figure it out, to regret his mistakes and come crawling back to her. She should have never dated anyone that stupid.

The story of Aunt Kalliope's vengeance upon her estranged lover was a famous family tale. A curse from the eye is a bad day; a curse from the head is a bad event. A curse from the heart is death, slow and painful, the physical manifestation of the death of love itself.

He was crying now, gut wrenching sobs. The sound was familiar. She had cried those sobs before, many times over.

A year and a half.

Even after so long, she could still feel the words in her mouth. She had whispered them aloud, three times. A whisper—all she was brave enough to manage. His heart would bleed for her as hers had bled for him.

To kakosu, to kero.

To kakosu, to kero.

To kakosu, to kero.

She picked up the phone. Pressed three numbers.

"9-1-1 emergency."

"There's a dead man on my front porch."

There was one last bang on the door. His hand slid down the glass, leaving a trail of bright red blood.

Allie sighed, and then gave the woman her address.

She was still cleaning up his messes.

POCKET FULL OF POSEY

"All those bitches need to die."

"Now, now, Rosalyn. These were all the people who were cruel to you in high school?"

"The nine—well, ten—people the planet would be better off without, yes."

"You can't still feel that way. You haven't seen most of them in ten years."

"Google is an amazing tool, Dr. Ford."

The psychiatrist chuckled and sat her legal pad on the tasteful mahogany and glass table beside her chair. *I probably bought that table*, thought Rosalyn, *and that chair*. Dr. Ford crossed her legs, leaned forward, and clasped her hands. Rosalyn braced herself for whatever stupid idea was about to slide off that silver tongue insurance companies had shelled out so much for on her behalf over the last decade-plus. Silly as those ideas were, though, Rosalyn still took Dr. Ford's advice more often than not. All those mundane sociology experiments were multivitamins for her soul; Rosalyn swallowed them with a large grain of salt (and sometimes a lime chaser). They were her church on Sunday, her good deeds for the week/month/year, and once accomplished she was free to move about the rest of her life with a light heart. Light-er. Less dark than normal.

Dr. Ford's smile showed off eighty-three percent of her professionally-whitened teeth. "You need to go to this reunion."

"I need world peace too, but you don't see that happening."

"The first step to world peace is making peace with yourself."

Rosalyn sighed. It was always a losing battle, not that she played to win. "You want me to walk into the lion's den."

"I want to prove that there is no lion's den. There never was."

Every muscle from the top of Rosalyn's head to the tip of her toes went stiff. What kind of professional talk was that? How could she say that *knowing* what hells Rosalyn had walked through every day at Freedom High? "I can't. Not alone."

"But you won't be alone…" Rosalyn raised an eyebrow. She was trying to weasel out of the event, not ask for a date. "…you have Posey," Dr. Ford finished.

Rosalyn couldn't help but smile at the name, and she pulled Posey out of her purse. Aunt Jo and Uncle Dickie had given her the darling gnome keychain on her fifteenth birthday. Gnomes had always made her smile, that in itself such a rarity that her father landscaped a garden in which she could display her collection. Posey was one of the few female gnomes. She had a fat daisy on her little red hat, a golden monkey on her shoulder, and a red cap mushroom in her arms. The irony that this symbol of purity and cuteness was ready to poison her enemies at a moments' notice was what Rosalyn loved best.

For Dr. Ford, Posey embodied all the loved ones Rosalyn admired and never wanted to disappoint. Posey was a cute, dangerous, portable conscience that held the keys to Rosalyn's getaway car.

"I have Posey," Rosalyn repeated dutifully.

"You'll be fine," said Dr. Ford.

"I'll be food for the wolves," said Rosalyn.

"There are wolves in the lion's den?"

Rosalyn nodded. "And they all have sharp teeth." Dr Ford laughed again, from the belly, shoulders shaking; the genuineness of it startled Rosalyn and made her wonder briefly if her shrink was having a seizure. "What's funny?"

"Oh, Rosalyn. You have what all of us wish we had at our high school reunions: you're beautiful, successful, and not a little bit famous. Anyone who didn't know your name then certainly knows it now."

True enough. If they couldn't afford any of the Rosey-O high-end-nano hair product line, then they'd seen her on the covers of magazines, or the guest appearance on *Whoopi*, or splashed across the rags at the grocery store self-checkout lines. The scandal had been viral, proving the WorldWideGrapevine could still propagate faster than any biotech.

The hair products had started out as many other things do—a laugh, a lark, payback on the science teacher her freshman year that suggested that ridiculous fair project on hair dye. Add some punk, Manic Panic, nanotech, a few too many Starbucks Vitamin Waters, and far too little sleep. It was inevitable for two genius roommates to come up with a nano-enhanced, programmable hair dye. It was also inevitable that Natasha—high on Water and the rush of completion—had tried the test batch too soon. The nanites affixed themselves to every hair follicle on her skin, entering her body and then her bloodstream and into her brain far too quickly. Natasha had lived long enough to sneeze and ask Rosalyn for a tissue.

Dr. Ford had taken on double-duty as grief counselor, the 4.0 was followed immediately by an offer from an overly-caffeinated venture capitalist, and the rest was history the lawyers made sure Rosalyn never had to talk about again.

"…must be *someone* you want to see after all these years," Dr. Ford was saying.

"Josie." The word popped out of Rosalyn's mouth without asking permission, which Rosalyn would have denied. After all those years, the two syllables still broke her heart.

"Ah," was Dr. Ford's professional reply. "So here's what I want you to do."

"Beyond walking through the doors?"

"Oh my, yes. I want you to go down this list and say hello to each person on it. You don't have to swap cookie recipes or cry on each other's shoulders; just a polite salutation. That's all."

Rosalyn took The Kill List back from Dr. Ford and gingerly folded it along the deep creases made with rage so long ago. She didn't have to look again at the rounded handwriting in a variety of colored inks; she knew every name by heart. Rosalyn wondered how many other shrinks were returning similar lists to emo kids of the aughties and suggesting they make amends. "You are a cruel woman, Dr. Ford."

"You wouldn't have me any other way."

***

Rosalyn slid her sapphire green Jaguar into the farthest parking space from the clubhouse. Her father, who'd spent large amounts of time in Afghanistan before the occupation ended, had taught her to always have an eye on her exit strategy. It was a hard habit to break, and so far one Dr. Ford hadn't asked her to.

She took three deep breaths, slid on her strappy black Dakota Fanning heels, and adjusted her enormous Lady Gaga sunglasses. A decade ago she'd walked the halls at Freedom High in black lipstick, a fuchsia lace tutu, and rainbow knee socks. Now, she opted for low-key: a simple black dress and one of her least ostentatious necklaces. Ironically, it was a large lacquer cross on a raw silk burgundy choker. If this did turn into a gang hit, she could at least use it as a weapon in a pinch. She smoothed down her shoulder-length, straight, brown hair. It was only colored with a now out-of-date version of the Rosie-O nanites that only made the ends black, as if they'd been dipped in ink. Thanks to Rosalyn, brown hair was now quite the rarity among humans within her own income bracket. She figured she was going to stick out like a sore thumb anyway; she certainly wasn't going to look like she was trying.

She beeped her car locked and kissed Posey for good luck before dropping her keys into her tiny Bieber clutch. She could do this. She could totally do this. And when it all went down in flames, she always had her exit strategy. Thanks, Daddy.

The first pair of glass doors she tried to the clubhouse was locked, and she refused to call it a sign. She marched all the way to the front of the building intently, like she was walking a Paris catwalk. There was Daisy Scofield, standing behind the welcome table, twenty months pregnant and beaming like sunshine. Anyone else would be high on Starbucks decaccinos, but Daisy Scofield had been beaming like that since she'd popped out of her own mother's womb. She gave Rosalyn a smile that would have knocked Dr. Ford over at twenty paces, and Rosalyn was glad she still had on her sunglasses.

"Rosie Posie Pudding Pie, kissed the girls and made—"Daisy slapped a hand over her traitorous mouth and a cloud went over the sun.

"A girl always wants to be remembered for her accomplishments," Rosalyn said as she scanned the HELLO, MY NAME IS stickers on the table between them. She let the glasses slide down her nose and gave Daisy a lusty wink. "I still make girls cry."

Daisy giggled behind her hand and then gasped when she saw which sticker Rosalyn had slapped to her chest. "Silly Rosie. Now what do I do if Susan San Giovanni decides to show up?"

"You didn't hear? Murdered, poor thing. Her husband snapped, killed her and her children in their sleep, and then hung himself. They said it was some sort of Warcraft PTSD episode or something. I'm wearing the nametag in her honor."

Daisy's cornflower blue eyes brimmed with tears. "Oh my. I didn't know. Bless her heart. Yes, you should wear the nametag. She would have liked that. I'll say a prayer for her."

Rosalyn patted Daisy on the shoulder and continued down the main hall. She hoped Susan SanGiovanni did show up. There was a shortage of good stories in the world.

Rosalyn smirked at the screamingly happy sign some mad scrapbooker with access to Photoshop and too much glue— possibly Daisy—had assembled so that no one mistook what was behind Doors Number One and Two for anything other than the Best Reunion EVAR. Rosalyn wrapped strong fingers with perfectly manicured nails around the handle and pulled.

What was actually behind the doors was a nightmare. Honestly, Rosalyn was pretty sure she had woken in a cold sweat from a scene just like this. Towers of fruit posed by chocolate fountains and lukewarm egg rolls smiled at her from their warming trays. A line started at the canditini bar and wrapped halfway around the room, and Christina Leffler serenaded the far-too-sober assembly with a stirring rendition of Ke$ha's *Tik Tok* on the Wii Sing like she was performing on New Year's Eve in Times Square.

Rosalyn glanced down to make sure she was still wearing clothes. Check. This was for real, all right.

In a class of over five hundred students there were only about fifty people in the room; leave it to the student council members of 2010 to make their own reunion list exclusive. Nitwits. They were all there, the entire Kill List from A to Z, all shiny and happily ignorant of how much Rosalyn's palms itched for a gun with nine equally shiny bullets.

Number Nine: Scott Ziwicki. Scott always stayed in last place in every incarnation of The Kill List because Rosalyn liked the completeness of ending the list with Z. Scott had been one of the first names, though, as he originally coined the "Rosie Posie Pudding Pie" rhyme. The acclaimed lyricist had gone on to pen several horrible novels starring a female protagonist named Rosie Pye. He probably never would have been published had Rosalyn herself not gone on to such fame and infamy.

Number Eight: Thuy Vu. Terminally petite Thuy had broken

Rosalyn's pencil in the second grade, causing Rosalyn to retaliate and slap the wretched vandal. They were both ushered to the principal's office, one of the only times Rosalyn was ever called into the principal's office. It scarred her for life. After that, she made a point of never getting caught.

Number Seven: Brendan Lee. Brendan had been caught multiple times cheating off Rosalyn's tests, but the teacher never moved him. He always wore a sneer every time Rosalyn was around, like he'd just smelled rotten eggs.

Number Six: Nick Smith. Nick's transgression was that he was totally obsessed with Rosalyn. The puppy dog love might have been flattering at one point, until the day he realized he was going nowhere with her and turned everything he knew about her into jabs and jokes.

Number Five: Mrudula Rue. The bitch touched her iPod. TWICE. Nuff said.

Number Four: Mark and Amanda Owen. The siblings, close enough in age to be in the same grade, were each only annoying enough to merit half a spot on the List. Mark was the class clown, which meant nothing that crossed his path was sacred. Amanda always had one ear attached to the phone, and there was usually a boy on the other end. If she wasn't talking to the boy, she was talking about the boy. And she had an unnatural addiction to corn dogs.

Number Three: Aimee Branson. Head cheerleader and Class Secretary. Far too beautiful to give anyone the time of day. She had only ever turned up her pert little nose at Rosalyn. Rosalyn still remembered how perfectly balanced her nostrils were, even when flared.

Number Two: Christina Leffler. Christina always had to be center stage, always had to have the spotlight. She'd gone so far as to YouTube Rosalyn during her audition for the High School play. Rosalyn was a laughing stock, and Christina got the solo. Christina always got the solos.

Number One: Ariell Bublé. Back in elementary school, Ariell had been one of her very bestest friends. She and Rosalyn and Josie Camire had been the Three Musketeers. They shared everything from cupcakes to gum. They finished each other's sentences. They knew each other's passwords. They were inseparable. And then one day, out of the blue, Ariell walked up to Josie and Rosalyn and announced that she couldn't be friends with them anymore, because she was going to be friends with Aimee and Christina and Thuy. Rosalyn was only slightly less devastated that day than she was a week later, when Ariell read Rosalyn's diary out loud in front of the whole cafeteria. The teacher caught her and made her stop, but not before everyone had heard the dramatic scene about Josie and Rosalyn kissing in the closet. Ariell had been there too, but as the reader, had conveniently edited herself out of the scene.

And there she was, on the other side of the dance floor, perfect as a princess in a pink chiffon dress with matching streaks like ribbons in her long champagne blonde hair. She chatted prettily with Thuy and someone on the wait staff. Mark pressed an orange post-it to the waitress's back. Amanda stood behind him, eating all the crescent rolls. Nick sidled up to the buffet table with her and sexually harassed the ice sculpture. Rosalyn's heel hit the cheap linoleum of the dance floor and she froze. Her stomach cramped. She wasn't ready. She couldn't do it. Not yet.

Luckily, she didn't have to. A petite ball of squee came barreling toward her, an afro of rainbow curls flashing like a bad acid trip. Rosalyn noted that Aimee Branson had splurged for the glitter upgrade to her hair pyrotechnics. Or her husband, Rosalyn noted as the rock on Aimee's left hand dug into Rosalyn's back.

"Oh-em-gee, I was driving myself crazy hoping that you'd come. And I am so glad you did! You have totally made my year! I love you!" Aimee squeezed tighter—her perky implants were as rock hard as her wedding ring. "Look!" Aimee affected an even higher pitch as she showed the diamond off and answered Rosalyn's unasked question. "It's Aimee Lee now. Brendan and I got married!"

"Confused" was an understatement. She and Aimee had not been BFFs. And Brendan? Really? Three and seven on The Kill List; a perfect ten now together in wedded bliss. Vomit-worthy, to be sure. Rosalyn glanced over Aimee's shoulder and through her neon stripper curls to see Brendan, the ruby pinstripe of his suit mirrored in his dark hair and goatee. Chameleon expansion pack. Nice. And not a sneer to be found. He was checking out Rosalyn's ass instead. She barely recognized him without his nose crinkled in disgust.

Rosalyn felt lightheaded and looked around for video cameras. Of course, had there been any, Christine would have either been in front of them, or directly behind them. Since she was moving from her last song right into Train's "Soul Sister," Rosalyn figured she was safe from any sort of spotlight.

Aimee seemed to be waiting for Rosalyn to say something, so she said, "Congratulations!" and hugged them both. She then crossed her arms in front of her, pinching the inside of one elbow to make sure she was still part of reality. Aimee launched into how many children she had, and what she was doing now. Something with curtains. Between Christine's crooning and the roaring in her ears, Rosalyn couldn't be sure.

Aimee's frequency was like a homing device, and eventually it brought the entire Noxious Nine to the fore. Rosalyn didn't even have to seek them out; they all came to her. Another surprisingly unexpected development. They each hugged her warmly and started up conversations like there had never been ten years and a moat of hatred between them. They also crowded around her in a complete circle, claiming her as theirs and shielding her from the rest of the room. Rosalyn peeked between them and caught a glimpse or two of someone she might recognize, but every time she did, one of the Nine moved into her line of sight and asked her a silly question.

"Did you fly here from somewhere exotic?" asked Thuy. The nanites in her hair cascaded blue Vietnamese characters down the silken ebony length. Rosalyn secretly hoped they said, "Touch my hair and die, asshole."

"Yeah," Rosalyn answered. "Great Falls." Granted, she only kept her condo there for her visits with Dr. Ford.

"What was Whoopi like?" asked Mark. His pink hair matched his shoelaces. Rosalyn wondered if Mark had ever come out of the closet.

"Really funny, actually. My stomach hurt for days afterwards from laughing so much."

"What exciting adventures are you off to next? Exploring any new inventions? How's your love life?" Scott was as full of questions as he was of fecal matter. His hair was a dynamic mix of traditional blonde, brown, red, and gray that succeeded in being annoyingly eye-catching.

Rosalyn coyly answered frustration with frustration. "Nothing as wonderful as Rosie Pye, I'm sure. I shouldn't bore you with details."

"That's really a shame about Susan," Amanda said between mouthfuls of crescent roll.

Rosalyn patted her name tag sticker. "I was really broken up about it."

"Did you like my song?" asked Christina.

"You always were a nightingale," lied Rosalyn.

"How come you're not sporting any of the newest Rosie-O product?" asked Mrudula. Her hair slowly faded from blue to red, with her change in mood. "Don't you get all you want? Or was that not a perk of selling the formula?"

The truth wasn't something they wanted to hear. It never had been. "I much prefer seeing it on other people," said Rosalyn. "All of you wear it so well."

And they did, too. Each one of them, male and female alike, had one or more glitzy, ridiculously expensive, Rosie-O expansion packs. They all bragged about how many they had, as if competing for her affection, and the inventive ways they'd used them on everything from pets to naughty bits. Rosalyn drank the one or two neon canditinis that were handed to her. She didn't say much, just let them carry on selfishly about their shallow little lives. She laughed, but not with them.

Finally, Ariell put a thin, alabaster arm around Rosalyn. "Oh, how I've missed us," she said to the group.

"Me too," said Rosalyn, meaning something completely different.

As always, Dr. Ford had been right. There was no lion's den, and there were no wolves. There were only fish—large, silly, cheap carnival goldfish. They were born, grew up, married each other, had kids, and never left the pond of Northern Virginia. It may as well have been small town Kentucky for all that gene pool multiplied. Only people who stepped outside the fishbowl realized how small it was. These popular people weren't fat and bald, like the clichés had her hope for; they were all still just as beautiful as Rosalyn remembered. But they were also sad. This tiny little goldfish bowl was all they would ever know, and all they cared to know. Dead or alive, it didn't really matter in the long run. This small, small world was the fate to which they were doomed.

Rosalyn pitied them. And three seconds after that, she wanted to escape from their suffocating embrace. She knew if she cried "potty," the girls would all come with her; such was the way of the herd. So she faked a vibrating phone and excused herself out to the hallway to return her very important imaginary call. She scooted past Daisy, who had taken a break from her table and was peeking through the doorway at the festivities.

"They haven't changed a bit," Rosalyn assured her.

"Most people never do," Daisy said with a sigh.

Rosalyn wasn't technically lying—she actually had missed a few texts from Kelli Keene, her new bestest-bestest. Kelli made sure, in very few words and no uncertain terms, that Rosalyn knew exactly what she was missing by not hurrying up to join her in the Cayman Islands. Kelli also sent two pictures: one of a strawberry daiquiri with a ridiculous amount of fruit, and one of her getting frisky with a cabana boy. Rosalyn wasn't jealous. Much. She'd done what she'd needed to do, and she'd be on her way soon enough. She better be. The next message would be a video, featuring more Kelli and fewer clothes. That was typically her M.O.

She made a quick pit stop in the bathroom, closing the door on the outside world and reveling in the quiet. She had a longstanding tradition of hiding in bathrooms: one of the habits that Dr. Ford had made her stop. Rosalyn figured she'd be forgiven this once. Conquering the Noxious Nine was a big step.

She walked to the sinks, placing her palms down against the cool counter. She looked in the mirror, tore off her stupidly huge sunglasses, and looked again. She was not one of them. She never had been. Making money and being famous didn't make her one of them. Their pretending that she was and making a big show didn't make her one of them either. Once upon a time, that's all it would have taken, and maybe, in their little fishbowl world, that's still all it took. But not in hers. Rosalyn would walk away from this building and never look back.

She turned the faucet in front of her on full blast and thrust the ends of her hair beneath the water, washing every bit of the nanite blackness down the drain until there was nothing left but brown. Brown old Rosalyn. Pure Rosalyn and nothing else. She dried it off with a handful of paper towels. She spun around in the mirror and looked over her shoulder, making sure it was all gone, making sure that there wasn't a sign on her back left by Mark. Or a knife left by

Ariell. She took a Burt's Bees Shimmer from her purse and applied it with a shaky hand.

"If you've got a stash of that stuff, it's more precious than gold," a voice said from behind her. "I can't find Shimmers anywhere anymore."

Rosalyn adjusted her eyes to focus on Josie. There in the mirror they were together, just like they'd never been apart. Her soft eyes were still green as olive branches, complementing the ice green frosting on the layered ends of her hair that curved around her heart-shaped face. Her Cupid's bow lips curved up into a smile. She was a vision come to life, ten times more beautiful than Rosalyn had ever dreamed.

"Take it." Rosalyn turned and offered Josie the slender yellow tube of Shimmer. Josie did not disappear; she was right there in flesh and blood. But everything was different now. They had both moved on. That close friendship, that everlasting bond between them, had only lasted as long as it took for the teal Sharpie in her yearbook to dry. Even standing here in 3-D, Josie was still a memory, a picture in a wallet, a tag on a FaceSpace album.

"Thank you," said Josie, who also seemed to be at a loss for words. The lines of communication went both ways; it hadn't been only her fault that the two of them had grown apart. Rosalyn wasn't here to build bridges or heal old wounds. She and Josie just hadn't been meant to be. And that was that. Life goes on.

Rosalyn cupped Josie's face in her hand and kissed her on the cheek. "You look good," she whispered. Despite the cupid's-bow smile, a fat tear escaped and slid between Rosalyn's fingers. Without another word, Rosalyn left the bathroom slightly proud of herself.

She still had it.

"Leaving so soon?" asked Daisy as Rosalyn passed by her table again.

"I have to meet someone," explained Rosalyn. "I could really only stop in for a minute."

Daisy held up a hand. "No explanation necessary. I'm just glad you came at all. It's really nice to see you, Rosalyn."

Why hadn't she and Daisy been closer? Rosalyn tried to think back, but memory escaped her. Not that it mattered. What mattered to Rosalyn was the here and now. Daisy's optimism, remarkable enough back then, was in this decade more rare and precious than crude oil. Rosalyn reached into her bag. "A picture for old time's sake?"

Daisy smiled and snuggled into the crook of Rosalyn's arm as she deftly flipped the camera around to take a vanity shot of them both. The flash was only slightly brighter than Daisy's smile.

"Gosh, Rosalyn. That flash… I think I'm blind."

"One more time," said Rosalyn. "I think I blinked." That's right. One more time with the hidden EM pulse for good measure, just to make sure every nanite left on Rosalyn's and Susan's bodies was rendered completely inert. The Rosie-O product she'd worn in had been old, one of the very first incarnations, from a stash she'd secreted away for a time such as this.

Rosalyn called it version 4.0.

She air-kissed Daisy and wished her luck with her baby—or however many babies were brewing in that enormous belly. She dropped the "camera" back into her purse and rummaged for her keys, finding them before she reached the exit doors. She popped the red cap of Posey's mushroom up with her thumbnail, slid the pad of her finger over the tiny button there…and froze.

Josie. Gods, she'd touched Josie in the bathroom. She'd washed the 4.0 nanites out of her hair by then, but there was no way to be sure Josie didn't get any on her. In fact, she was 100% sure that she couldn't be sure. That was the whole point of having the EM camera. But it was too late to turn back to find her. It had been too late for about a decade now.

Rosalyn pushed the button.

She stood at the doors, staring outward, just long enough to hear a sneeze. Then she pushed through them and calmly strode the length of the parking lot to her getaway vehicle. In twenty minutes she'd be on a private jet to the Caymans, unburdened and free, and this shiny little fishbowl would be nothing but a headlight in the rearview mirror, another anonymous star in the sky.

She'd miss Dr. Ford.

The Way of the Restless

Electronic doorbells jangled. Elvis sashayed into the diner, took a stool at the antiseptic orange counter, and ordered a cherry pie.

"Ain't got cherry today hon." Cayenne absentmindedly wiped the cracked enamel with a damp rag; she didn't take her eyes off the iVizion soap for a second. Nikki and Victor were apparently on the outs. Again. Heated argument. Always the way of the restless: on again, off again for the last few centuries. Elvis knew a bit about that. Sure, Dot had always made a scene, shrieked mercilessly, and thrown whatever was at hand, but the day she'd left for good she'd just turned and walked away without a word. The way they were going at it, Nikki and Victor would be back together again before the end of the daymonth.

No one could have guessed that soap operas would be the biggest outlet for legalized cloning. Elvis wasn't sure if that was a good thing or a bad thing, not that he had any right to complain. He caught his reflection in the glass of the pie case and resisted the urge to snarl. Had some distant grandmother not been ready, willing, and fertile when they'd finally dug up The King all those years ago, he wouldn't even be here.

He spread his fingers on the slick counter before him, orange as ration crackers. Orange as surplus flight suits. Dot's flight suit. Nope. Not going there.

"Sweet potato then," he said, when Nikki took a dramatic breath.

Something slightly less orange.

Cayenne's eyes remained glued. "Case is stale, shug. Go pull a fresh one out of the back?"

"Anything for you darlin'," he drawled. Straight to business then. He was fine with that. Elvis dismounted and made his way through the swinging doors to the back office.

Jane was smoking. Jane was always smoking. Being a Phytollan refugee, Jane had managed to swindle a medicinal scrip for nicotine and a license to smoke in public. Elvis suspected it was more of an affectation than a need, but he had to admit that her skin did look healthier when the tint ran more green than blue. And of course, Jane could swindle anything, any day of the week. That's what she had him for.

Swindler, driver, persuader, seducer, anarchist, requisitionist, treasure hunter, bounty hunter, collector, seller. Elvis had acquired more than a few job titles during his time with Jane. Good thing he didn't bother with business cards. Nobody on Jane's payroll did. Not that he knew anyone else on her payroll, or wanted to. He could, however, guess Miles Draven was behind that box of Cubans so proudly displayed on her desk. Draven was good. He was better.

Elvis extracted the small velvet pouch, soft like skin, from one of the many pockets in his black leather pants and tossed it onto the ledger Jane refused to look up from. She took a long drag on her cig and exhaled slowly out her three nostrils before setting her pen down. She sniffed the bag—how she could smell anything beyond that cloud of smoke was beyond him—and then slid the contents into her palm. The mother of pearl on the cameo glittered beneath her unforgiving desk lamp. "Catherine Rainey," she said with a voice like gravel. "Nice to meet you."

"The Library of Robinson 7 is now vacant."

"Take the ghost out of the ghost town and what do you get?" Jane mused. "Some would call it genocide."

"I call it a job well done," said Elvis. "You wanted a planet, you got one."

Jane closed her fingers over the Librarian's shining face. "Did she give you any trouble?"

Sensor rats. Laser spray. Acid cannons. That unrelenting, cold winter gray. Elvis shrugged. "Nothing out of the ordinary." Nothing but that soft voice, repeating the same sad tale over and over again. He shoved that memory back, swept it under the fluorescent orange carpet in the bowels of his mind. "The hard data storage is still intact. Her access memory might be damaged, though; she was rambling when I got there. Spent enough time rerouting systems to realize it was on a cycle. I recorded the message to a beacon and left it there transmitting so no one'd be the wiser, but I suggest that your customer to plants their flag soon." A lost city. An entire planet up for grabs. He wondered which refugee camp had been the highest bidder in that room. He had a sudden image of a city full of Janes, walking around care free in their blue-green birthday suits, sucking down a bilious atmosphere of nicotine and schadenfreude. Jane, who had said something. "Sorry. What?"

"What. Was. The. Message," she said slowly.

"I wasn't paying that much attention," he lied. "Something about her daughter."

Jane said nothing, didn't even nod, but Elvis took the bounce of the cig between her thin lips as acknowledgement. Mission accomplished. On to the next thing. "I've got something, but you're not going to like it," she said, waiting on the platform when his ship of thought landed.

She was usually right. The announcement still piqued his interest, though. He'd hate whatever she was about to ask him to do, but it would no doubt leave him with at least a Buchanan Cycle's worth of bar tabs in decent stories. "I'll take it."

"Fine," said Jane to her ledgers. "Skeezix is your contact."

Aw, *Hezmat*, Elvis cursed in Venutian. Skeezix. No-good, thieving, tweaked-out son of a port skank. Backstabbing, bastard mutt of a blinking alien whose chameleon hide was more trouble than it was worth, and whose meter-long tongue was as silver as it was forked. Elvis hadn't seen Skeezix since…since that last run with *her*. He was surprised anyone had let him live this long.

Jane raised a thin eyebrow. "And he's currently in the diner eating your pie."

Nice to know some things hadn't changed. Elvis burst back through the swinging door in time to watch Skeezix lick the last of the whip cream off the plate with that acrobatic tongue.

"Thanks, E." Skeezix burped, his dull orange lips betraying the pumpkiny sweetness that had just passed through them. "Cayenne, my loveliest, you've outdone yourself. Haven't had something that good in a daymonth of forevers. Still can't top that messberry cobbler Dot used to make, though." He had obviously been hoping for a reaction from Elvis, and he got one. "Wow. I guess I can see now why that expression became famous. Dot's still a sore spot, huh? You know, you should really give her a call. You two were—"

"What's the job, Skeezix." The last person he'd confess his deep dark secrets to would be a snitch.

"No time to cut chase. I see how it is," said Skeezix. "Well, this is easy leezy. Art heist. In and out job."

"What do you need me for, then?"

"Not me," said Skeezix, "my employer. I'm just a messenger, same as you, only shorter and better looking. And full of pie." Elvis refused to react, so Skeezix went on. "Frame is in a safe in the cargo hold of your basic Grub-run interstellar transport. I imagine there will be quite a few other goodies in there too." He waggled his eyebrows, but Elvis didn't bite there either. He flipped open the electronic assistant on his wrist and punched a few buttons. "Well don't get distracted. You're only there for the art. I'm downloading the location and lot number onto your EA. You're the systems guy. Should be the breeze for you."

Elvis confirmed the transfer and nodded. "Where do I make the drop?"

"Where else?"

Elvis looked at his EA again. "You're kidding me." He remembered that warehouse in the Colt Islands all too well. Skeezix's main hideyhole, back in the day. Back on the day that Dot had strung him up and left him there, the heartless wench.

Skeezix grinned a disturbing pointed-toothed smile the width of his face. "Good times."

"Let's just get on with it," said Elvis. "How far can you take me?"

Skeezix laid a clawed hand on his shoulder and Elvis felt the world bend around him as they blinked out of the diner. When they "landed," he swallowed multiple times in quick succession as his stomach did backflips. He hated when Skeezix blinked him without warning, but he instantly stopped lamenting his stolen pie. As much as he despised it he stared at Skeezix, willing his bearings to right themselves. When they did he realized that the snitch's orange blush had faded into the gunmetal gray of the cargo hold around them.

"Delivery in thirty seconds or less," said Skeezix. "Have fun!"

"Whoa," said Elvis as the world slowly stopped spinning. "You can't just leave me here." To which Skeezix responded by blinking out and proving him wrong. Elvis cursed in Wyvernese. Skeezix's face may change with the weather, but Elvis had no doubt his belly stayed yellow. He shook his head. Some people never changed. He wasn't sure if that was a good thing or a bad thing either.

The first thing he did was use his EA watch to hack into the comms system. It took him less than five minutes of listening to realize that the ship he was on was transporting more than just nonsentient cargo. However, it only took him a moment of shuddering vibrations to realize that the ship he was on was currently taking off. Elvis cursed again, this time in Candician. He was only fluent in three languages, but he could get by in a solid dozen and boasted invectives in at least twice that. It was always good to know what the customer was calling you behind your back.

One thing at a time. There was no stopping the ship now, and no point. First, he needed to find the painting and liberate it from the safe. He'd worry about how to get out of there when there was an out to actually get to. Elvis brought up the location numbers and cross-checked them on the ship's manifest, running the program in diagnostic mode to avoid detection. It took him longer to locate the shipping container than it did to disarm the securities and crack the safe. Like Skeezix had said in his own rare brand of tweaked-out vocabulary, it was easy leezy. Perhaps too easy leezy.

Elvis coded the locks back into place, resealed the container, and dragged the waist high polymer crate back to his listening post at the comms unit. He had passed the hibernation chambers on the way to find the artifact and, now that he had the luxury to be, he was curious as to their contents. Based on the mode of transport and the level of secrecy around them he had his own idea as to the origins, so he was not surprised when it was confirmed. Eddys. Anarchist groups who frequented the fringes of the galaxies, refusing to ally themselves with any defined place or government. The only commonality was that they were all misfits, on the basis of which some incredibly strong bonds between sects had been created. So strong, in fact, that certain planets felt threatened and paid a great sum to see the nomad Eddy groups "taken care of." If he'd had the means, he'd get them out, hand them all weapons, and set them free on their captors.

Don't get distracted, Skeezix's voice echoed in his head. *You're only here for the art.* Elvis sneered. Oh, like hell. He was here for himself. He pulled up the codes for the hibernation chambers—a bit more strenuous task this time—and checked the numbers against his watch. Something was off. He altered his approach, reentered the sequence, and checked again. No…the numbers were right. The calculations were the same. But the results the ships computer was spewing forth were not in Grub units of relative time.

Elvis had become a bit of an expert on timepieces after the accident, and the emergency installation of Dot's artificial gearheart. Her atomic ticker, that's what she'd called it. That had been the beginning of the end, and he knew it. He had never forgiven himself for putting her in harm's way. He couldn't let her keep taking the risks she kept taking without company or comment, and boy did she let him have it. Perhaps she had thought it flattering at first, but she never had been the fragile flower. Dot Stringer was a star on the brink of nova vaccu-sealed in a can of worms and whupass with "Trouble" stamped on the label and woe to any man who opened it.

Gods, how he'd loved her.

He shook it off. The proper shift equations always had to be downloaded into the gearheart prior to any jump so that it could equalize immediately upon landing. A blink like the one Skeezix had pulled on him earlier had the potential to kill her. And so Elvis had become familiar with possibly even more alien units of time than he knew curses. He wasn't positive what these units were, but they were not Grub units. And if they were not Grub units, then they must belong to the only other race of beings on the ship…the beings in the hibernation chambers that currently appeared to be decompressing. It seemed that the Eddys had beaten him to the punch and already planned their own mutiny.

Aw, *Hezmat*.

The relief that he was no longer escorting scores of innocent anarchists to their death was suddenly buried under self-preservation. He laid the polymer crate flat on the floor and casually sat on top of it. He waited patiently while faction after faction of Eddys awoke, struggled in lungfuls of the hold's stale air, mustered, and armed themselves. And when the nomad leader strode up to him, he raised his hands in surrender.

"Impressive," said Elvis. "That was the quickest hibernation recovery I believe I've ever witnessed."

"Training goes a long way," said the nomad leader, "as does the right combination of stimulants." He lowered his wave weapon at Elvis's head. "Tell me why I shouldn't kill you."

"I'm just here for the art," Elvis said automatically, and then thought better of it. He snapped the fingers of one surrendering hand and pointed at the nomad leader. "I can give you the coordinates of a newly-vacant planet in the Robinson System."

"How do I know you're not lying?"

Elvis shrugged. "You don't."

The nomad leader motioned with his gun. "Punch in the coordinates. We'll see when we get there."

"When I turn out to be right, I'll need free passage back off the rock. I want a ship and—he knocked on the crate beneath him—this box. The planet's yours." As was whatever fallout came later when the high bidders showed up to claim it. Or when the Asteroid Spiders came out of hibernation. Surely nothing a seasoned Eddy general hadn't been through before.

The nomad leader lowered his weapon. "If there's a ship to be had, friend, it's yours."

There were, in fact, ships to be had on Robinson 7. Elvis had already picked one out. A cherry red rocket, far classier than that ancient, energy-swilling Star-V. Dot refused to trade in. The keys were already in his pocket. "Then I believe you have a ship to take over," said Elvis.

He stayed in the hold for that part. He didn't watch them execute the crew, but he did felt the vibration of the wave weapons, and he fell off the crate when they opened a starboard airlock and the ship shifted beneath him. In the light of the now-empty hibernation chambers, he could make out something etched just over the seam. Words. He squinted. No…just one word. A word he was definitely familiar with, in one of the languages that he just so happened to speak fluently. He ran his thumb over the ragged edges.

ELVIS.

It took him far too long to find something with which to break the seal and pry open the crate. Once he had he found another crate inside, and then layers upon layers of protective wrapping. The actual frame was much smaller than the polymer crate had led him to believe. He held it out before him and looked into an older version of himself, in a white jumpsuit on black velvet. He stared at it for a long time, marking the differences in the face of the ancient singer, examining the freeform shapes behind him like clouds of space dust that resolved themselves into a guitar, a neutron clock, an old film reel, a pair of sunglasses. This was more than just coincidence. Had to be. But why?

Elvis closed his eyes and tried to let the pieces fall into place, but he was distracted into holding himself steady while the ship began its planetary descent. Dot had always hated descent. "What's the point of flying if you have to land?" she'd say. Her earrings would rattle together like the open doors of the hibernation chamber, only at a higher pitch. She would hold his hand in one of hers and place the other one over her heart. Sometimes she'd leave her flight suit unzipped low enough to distract them both during the unpleasant experience. She liked to be watched, and she liked to know that it was him doing the watching. It would be a lifetime before he'd be able to get those pink, rhinestone-studded fingernails out of his mind, clashing against that ridiculous orange flight suit, sliding across her smooth skin, over her atomic ticker, and down…

Elvis opened his eyes and examined the painting again. He ran a hand across the soft velvet, soft like her skin, and over the face of the neutron clock. Neutron clock. Atomic ticker. It wasn't much of a stretch. Elvis picked up the frame and carefully crawled into the hibernation chamber where the light was better. He swept his hand one way across the clock, and then back the other way. The first essentially obliterated the face of the clock. The second revealed enough detail to make out the roman numerals. Only because he was looking for it did he find the tiny, five-pointed shape beside the number five. Star-V.

Elvis cursed in Fannish, Perkinese, Balsin, and Catawani, just for good measure.

When the Eddy ship finally landed, Elvis shook the nomad leader's hand in farewell beneath the ominous skies.

"There's one more thing I need."

The nanomaintained landscaping in front of the library had contained rainbow peonies, black-eyed susans, and a few other flowers he didn't know the names of. Not that he needed to know. Dot liked flowers, and the less ceremoniously presented the better. Ripped from a bed in a former ghost town should suit her just fine. He also relished the idea of giving her a black eye with some other woman's name on it. Dot liked irony too.

"Anything for you, my friend," said the nomad leader.

"Not for me," Elvis corrected. "For a girl. My girl."

The nomad leader smiled, grabbed the soldier that was standing closest to him, and hauled her up to his side. "I understand," he said, and with that she kissed him with a vigor that gave Elvis the perfect opportunity to walk away. Those two would be fighting again by the end of the week; if not themselves, then someone else. Off gain, on again; that was the way of the restless.

Elvis decided it was a good thing.

Savage Planet

Blu Valentine settled his cherry red rocket ship into position and held orbit. He watched Kat's fingers as she gently nudged the dial back and forth, her slender body concentrating on listening to whatever she thought she'd heard in the bright orange headphones that peeked out in slivers under her long dark hair.

Blu swiveled in his pilot's chair and bit the end of his pencil. He had a personal rule to have a pencil about his person at all times. It was good for gesturing, good for thinking, good for scribbling last-minute formulas in anti-grav, good for breaking when making a point, and a pretty good substitute for his tongue in most situations. He wiggled the bitter wood polymer between his teeth. "You're insane," he said.

"There is a voice out there. I swear."

"A beacon only dogs can hear," Blu muttered. "Kats too, apparently." He smiled. "Maybe it's a rogue veterinary post out here in the middle of—"

Kat released the dial long enough to reach out and smack him hard on the leg. Even considering the environmental suit he wore, she hit like a girl. He liked that about her. He swept her lithe frame with an appreciative glance. Truth be told, he liked quite a bit more than just that about her. He bit down hard on the pencil.

"I heard something…something about a sun. Or something near a sun? It had to have come from this planet. Brain On Board says its tilt indicates a highly eccentric orbit, possibly intersecting with a beta planet in the vicinity, both using that F1V dwarf star as their barycenter. Cycle around one more time, 'kay? Please. For my peace of mind."

"Katherine Savage, you and I both know that there are only two reasons for the existence of a beacon out here. BOB also says this starsforsaken rock is deserted, so I doubt it's a distress call. The second, and more appropriate reason, would be that it's a warning for passers-by to stay the hell away."

Kat sighed. "Maybe it's the first because someone is *stranded* on that starsforsaken rock. Or maybe it's the second and the beacon's malfunctioning. The Grub Whentime Contingent offers rewards for discovery and repair of such beacons, you know. Handsome rewards. Rewards big enough for your"—she turned her eyes away—"ship."

In his head, Blu heard another layer of her voice say "tarted-up bucket of bolts" at the same time another one echoed "ego" in that psychic harmony of hers which always set his teeth on edge. He still wasn't sure if she used her ability to get under his skin on purpose, or if she just ended up there from time to time by chance. "You sure it's not the beta planet we should be checking out? Maybe the signal's squibbled because it's coming from the other side of the star."

"No," smiled Kat. "It's this one." She pulled the headphone jack free, and a stream of garbled static filled the air. After a few seconds, a female voice distinctly said, "…*please find my daughter*…"

"Maybe it wasn't 'sun' after all," said Kat. "Maybe it was 'son.' If this woman's talking about her children, Blu, we have to find them."

***

This is Catherine Rainey, Librarian and last surviving entity of the planet known as Robinson Seven. Do not approach. But if you can hear my voice I beg you please, please find my daughter Samantha. I repeat: do not approach. There are spiders in the sun.

***

Kat couldn't remember the last time she had seen a flower. They spilled vibrantly down out of open windows here, ran rampant around man-sized boulders and over deserted roads, filled the cold mist with the thick scent of their strange honey. What had once been decorative landscaping was now a wilderness that rivaled even the Perkinese Pleasure Gardens.

The flowers told Kat many things. They spoke of a temperate climate, with sufficiently constant rainfall from the thick cloud cover. The clouds rolled playfully and quickly above her in shades of gray, with only a thin line of clear blue peeking out along the horizon. This foliage had been abandoned for at least a decade of Buchanan Cycles; before that. This planet had been much-beloved and reluctantly abandoned. Kat empathized, and felt an immediate kinship to this world. She took a deep breath, letting the fresh, fragrant air fill her lungs, asking the stars to let understanding seep through her pores, that the pollen of this world might remember what had happened and be hungry to tell her. She opened her eyes, resolutely unsatisfied.

Blu was staring at her breasts. She zipped up her jumpsuit as high as it would go and fired a glare at him. Let him think he was the cause of her disappointment. It wouldn't be the first time. If he hadn't been the quickest way out of the Springfield System, she never would have accepted his offer. He was far too handsome, a fact of which he was well aware, and which drew far too much attention. Her plan always had been—and still was—to desert him at the nearest outpost. Blu didn't need her—he had managed to survive perfectly well without her before now, and he would do so long after she was gone. He didn't need her. The thought was both a shame and a relief. As soon as she found a ship of her own, Kat would say goodbye. This planet just might be the place for such an opportunity.

She used her mental ability to keep Blu in love with her and frustrated by her in turns, just enough of the former to have him think her useful, and just enough of the latter to have him keep his distance. So far it had been a walk in the park. Caipira Lucille, the one-eyed witch who had raised her, had told her men were simple. Caipira Lucille had only been wrong about one thing in her life. It was not that.

Unfortunately, Caipira Lucille had not qualified the previous remark by saying that all women were smart. Had Kat been smart, she might never have stepped aboard that cherry red rocket ship in the first place. Had Kat been smart, she might have ignored that lone, static-riddled voice in the darkness. Had Kat been smart, she might have noticed the subtle movement out of the corner of her eye, the tiny shadow darker than those around it as it scurried between her feet, but she did not. She did not see the spider until it bit her. "*Ow!*"

To his credit, Blu had impressive reflexes. The spider, having discharged its duty, lived for but a brief moment before being crushed beneath Blu's sturdy boots.

"My hero," said Kat, rubbing her ankle. The nasty little vermin had somehow penetrated the layers of her environmental suit clear to the skin beneath. She scowled at the green, furry goo now stuck to Blu's sole. Serves it right.

"Better use the antivenom pen, just in case." She hesitated but he towered over her, refusing to let her take one more step away from the ship. "What, afraid it might take your sting out?"

Kat answered his laugh with her own, threw up her hands, and ducked back into the ship for the first aid kit. So maybe Blu wasn't stupid and selfish all the time. Just most of it. She pulled up the leg of her suit and pushed the pen into her ankle, the bite of the needle a whisper compared to the irritation left by the spider. She rubbed the skin briskly, feeling the area already becoming numb. Good. She ducked back out through the hatch, and was immediately knocked over by a pink dog.

"Wait!" she yelled before Blu could pull his wave pistol free of its harness. The dog—its flesh a deep red and the follicles of its hair a luminescent magenta—was now gobbling up two-no, three— more spiders Kat had not seen behind her. Deliberately or not, the dog had protected her by knocking her out of the way. After it finished gulping down the last furry leg, it barked—a loud, low bark that hummed in Kat's ears and resonated in the instinctive corner of her brain, the corner she called upon whenever she wanted to communicate without words. There was shuffling in the underbrush as a million hairy legs scattered.

"What is that thing?" asked Blu. He tilted his head. "It certainly wins the ugly prize."

It was friendly, latently psychic, and a natural predator to the little green alien arachnids that seemed unnaturally attracted to her. It could have been a hornbacked mizzling and Kat wouldn't have cared. Hell, if it knew how to fly a ship, Blu'd be on his own in a heartbeat. Kat ruffled the coarse fur on the dog's head. "He's my new best friend."

"Maybe he sent the signal," Blu said. "The one only dogs could hear. Which makes you a—"

"—a lovely and gracious young woman who will break your lower half into fourths if you even think of finishing that sentence. Now come on. BOB says the source of the beacon is this way." She made her way down the flower-choked road. Blu followed close behind. And, after a brief pause, the dog bound along after them.

***

This is Catherine Rainey, Librarian and last surviving entity of the planet known as Robinson Seven. Do not approach. But if you can hear my voice I beg you please, please find my daughter Samantha. I repeat: do not approach. There are spiders in the sun.

***

Blu stood frozen at the edge of the cobblestone square outside the humongous glass building that marked the City Center. Kat stood behind him, equally shocked, equally immobile, but more from the large pink dog that leaned against her leg and hummed a deep purr that rattled her bones. She turned her head this way and that, trying to locate the speakers from which the woman's voice now emanated, loud and clear, haunting and ominous.

Blu raised a hand. "Did she say spiders? She said spiders. Did you hear that?"

"In the sun," said Kat. "There is no sun. There are only stone shadows."

"There can't be stones with shadows without any sun. This cloud cover is already much sparser than it was."

"According to BOB, this planet's orbital cycle is approaching perihelion." Kat looked up from her wrist display. "It's Spring. We're heading closer to the star."

"Right," said Blu. "So we've got what…days? Months?" He slapped one of the large boulders that ringed the courtyard.

Kat remembered that thin line of blue sky on the horizon. Somewhere got sun today. She wondered if the diffuse shadow of the boulder on which Blu leaned was growing sharper, or if it was just her imagination.

"RAH!" he roared suddenly, lunging for her. Kat snapped out of her reverie, her concentration, and almost her skin. The pink dog barked and snapped at him; Kat secretly hoped it would accidentally tear his throat out. She punched Blu solidly on the shoulder. "Don't DO that," she scolded.

His wide smile carved dimples into those impudent cheeks. "Now let's find this warp-brained microphone hog and let her know that help has arrived. He leapt up the substantial flight of stairs to the front of the building in long strides.

As if in a dream, Kat watched the shadows before and after him grow substantially darker. A seam split in the clouds and the dying sun's rays burst through. The dog's hum-growl became a wild bark.

"*NO!*" Kat cried, but the word was drowned beneath the gnashing of teeth and the crunching of bone as the thing that had once been a stone enveloped Blu in a flurry of spindly legs, opened its huge jaws and snapped Blu's neck between them. She blocked everything out after that. Kat focused on running headlong for the glass doors of the Center, on the shrill bark of the pink dog that led the way, on the slap of her boot soles as they ran through the thick puddle of blood on the cobblestones.

***

The glass doors were automatic; there may have been some way to lock them, but Kat had no time to figure it out, no time to look back. The smell of blood choked her, but she had no time to be sick. She had no time to think about Blu apart from a fleeting wish that she had grabbed his wave pistol on her way past. She ran at full speed, following the pink dog up a wide, circular ramp. A bad decision, a worthless death, and she hadn't even witnessed that fabled rainbow. Kat felt cheated.

This is Catherine Rainey, Librarian and last surviving entity of the planet known as Robinson Seven.

Air burned in her lungs. How far up did this ramp go? She took a mental inventory of her defenses. She had fists, teeth, and feet. There was a knife strapped to the still numb calf beneath her flight suit, and the dog seemed to be a worthy adversary. Had they been up against only a handful of those green, furry annoyances like the one that had bit her in welcome, they may have had a chance. Against the giant monster that had attacked Blu, they stood significantly less of one. Against more…Kat didn't even bother entertaining that one. She needed the energy to run. And to plan. Only she had no real idea of what she was running from, and even less about where the pink dog was leading her.

If you can hear my voice I beg you please, please find my daughter Samantha.

"HELP!" Kat's raw voice echoed through the cavernous building. The monologue in the speakers was clear as a bell now.

There are spiders in the sun.

"PLEASE, HELP ME!" If the woman was somewhere inside this building, she had to hear that. The dog barked in exclamation on the same frequency, amplifying her cry for help on a subaudial level. A distress call only dogs could hear, Blu had said. The scream that burst from Kat's lips was one of laughter and grief and fear and exhaustion, each emotion vying for top note and all of them winning.

"I miss her with all my heart, with a heart I don't have, with whatever part of what's left of my soul that is still able to love."

"HELLO? IS ANYONE HERE?" Kat gasped for oxygen, choked on it. "Please," she begged.

"I miss her so much. Sometimes I think I can hear her voice, echoing down these empty halls…"

"It's me," Kat mouthed breathlessly, lacking the energy to scream. She and the pink dog burst through more glass doors at the top of the ramp. Kat folded in half and grabbed her knees, her body retching, her emotions still at war within. "It's me," she coughed. The pink dog leaned against her and Kat drew on his strength, forcing herself to remain standing.

The woman who stood before the windows on the observation platform slowly turned to face the room. Gray streaked her fair hair and wisdom lit her blue eyes, but there was a timelessness about her. Complete and utter timelessness. In the sky beyond the window at her back, the clouds parted and rolled together again in a ceaseless churn. A ray of sun caught the woman's cheek and shone right through her.

"Stars," the hologram cursed.

"Help me," said Kat.

"Initiate lockdown."

Kat heard invisible bolts slam home on the doors behind her, and down several alcoves around the room. She sagged to one knee, her sore leg finally unable to hold her.

"It is a bad time of year to be here," said the woman. "Not the worst, but not the best." Her image ghosted closer in a half-walk, half-glide. She examined the pair of them with her unblinking eyes. "Why are you here?"

"For you," said Kat. "Or, for who we thought was you. Or, for what we thought was who you used to be." She shook her head. The bizarre, circular ramblings of this woman who was no longer a woman, and yet a woman still, suddenly made sense.

The hologram tilted her head to indicate the dog. "We?"

"My…partner," said Kat. "He didn't make it."

"Lucky," said the woman. The evening light broke through again as the star sank toward the horizon, washing the underside of the roiling gray cloud cover with fiery pinks and yellows and reds. A mirror of blood on stone. Kat swallowed several times in quick succession, ordering her stomach to remain calm. The woman floated back over to the window. "Look," she beckoned.

Kat limped to the window and watched as each boulder, as far as the eye could see, stretched and uncurled itself in the waning light. The hollows of the stones became one, then two, then many dark legs, and the texture of the rock became fur. Each spider-like creature was easily twice the size of a man, with two rows of tinted, reflective eyes and formidable hinged mandibles, a featured they did not share with their lesser green cousins. Kat knew the incredible speed at which that unwieldy frame could move. She knew how efficiently those jaws could separate a man's head from his body. She refused to close her eyes; Blu would be there, dying before her all over again, as he had done during every blink between the front door and this mezzanine. So she kept them open, forced to watch the legions of giant alien spiders below wake from their hibernation.

It could have been worse, the woman had said. Yes, they might have landed on Robinson Seven at its perihelion, and not just on the Spring approach. Neither of them would have lasted long in the full sun. But BOB might have warned them of the presence of sentient life there. Maybe. Might. Could have. Shouldn't have. Whatever paths Kat had chosen in her life, they had all led her here. Now that she was here, she would deal with it. Just like she had always done.

"What is your name, child?"

Perhaps she was a child to this woman of indeterminate age. She felt as foolish, yet ancient in her present weariness. "Katherine Savage," she answered.

"I am a Catherine as well," the woman smiled. "Where is your ship?"

Kat gestured behind her without looking. "Back the way we came. Far back." So far back it seemed like miles. Years.

"What was your partner's name?"

"Blu," Kay said automatically. "Blu Valentine. It is—was—his ship."

"And what is your companion's name?"

Kat tore her gaze away from the Death at the window and looked at the pink dog who still leaned against her, humming into her bones. "I don't know. I don't—"she stumbled forward, catching herself on the glass. When she pulled her hand away, the print she left was smudged with blood. She didn't remember having touched any.

"He never told me either," said Catherine. "You have been bitten?" Kat had only the energy to nod in reply. "I was bitten too; I was the first victim. Became a prisoner in my own body. I offered to trade my consciousness and guard this facility in exchange for my daughter's passage off this planet. Once upon a time."

Catherine floated to a wall of flashing lights and dark monitors, at the center of which was embedded an ancient cameo of a woman with long, flowing hair, no doubt the vessel in which her consciousness had been stored decades ago. Kat shuffled slowly after her. "Touch the brooch," she said. Kat hesitated, and Catherine laughed. It was a strange sound, that laugh, so unpracticed as to almost sound disingenuine. "It has indeed been a long time since I have touched anyone, my child. But I assure you, I still know how." Kat still did not move. "You asked for my help. I am giving it to you if you are willing to take it." She tilted her head toward the window. "The Colony is waking. Do not squander what little time you have left."

Kat took a deep breath, exhaled slowly, and obscured the face of the beautiful cameo with the palm of her hand. The shell composite was cold to the touch, but warmed quickly to her hand. The hologram closed her eyes and flickered. Kat closed her eyes as well, concentrating on what she was feeling. Or, rather, what she wasn't feeling. Perhaps it had been too long since Catherine had been in contact with another human. Perhaps the venom in the spider's bite had already run its course through her system. Perhaps the vibrating purr of the dog by her side interfered with any sort of cellular interaction.

"Does your ship have a cryogenic, or some similar sort of hibernation chamber for long-distance travel?"

Her ship. It was not her ship. It was never her ship. "No," she answered. The dog barked. Catherine raised her eyebrows. "Then you will need to use your companion's ship. As I suspect you've noticed, the spider's poison has spread, but not irreversibly so. The antivenom has been helping, as has the dog. It is a slow mover, this one. It takes it time, damaging each and every cell beyond repair before moving on." Kat squeezed her eyes shut and watched Blu die again to distract herself from her own reality. "Hibernation might not be enough to stave it off, but it will slow the process even further. Record a message before you put yourself to sleep, and head for the nearest spaceport you know that has medical facilities."

"Will I make it?"

"You have to make it to the ship first," said Catherine. "But yes. There is a chance. If you do…"

"Yes?"

"If you do, please find my daughter." It was a fool's quest, but Kat had no other choice than to accept it.

"Samantha," said Kat. "I will. "She smirked. "If I make it."

"If you don't," said Catherine, "May you find peace in whatever gods' arms will hold you. But for now, those arms are mine. You may stand now."

Kat didn't realize she had sunk to her knee once again. She stood, and her strength surprised her. She felt awake and alive. She felt calm and collected. She felt…

"Invincible," Catherine supplied. "Now, go. Find her. Please. And take care of her." This last she said to the pink dog more than to Kat. "My daughter," she whispered after them as they left the room.

Kat followed the dog down winding corridors and darkened stairwells, its magenta hair glowing softly in the shadows. Catherine did well progressively unlocking doors before them and locking them back as they went along. Kat heard shuffling behind walls and on floors above and beneath them, softer than human footfalls, but more substantial than the pink dog's. There was a cloying scent in the air, a salty musk of dampness and dust that grew stronger the further down they traveled. Only once did a spider try to slam his body weight against a door to try and get at them, but they ignored it, continuing down the stairwell.

Kat had stopped praying a long time ago, but now she prayed that the doors would hold. She prayed that there would be no spider sentries watching for them to exit the building. She prayed that they would not be detected as they jogged through the forest of flowers around them and, when they were, she prayed that the synthetic strength Catherine had created within her would let her keep running.

She wondered how far away the dog's ship was. Had its masters landed during the sunny season? How had the dog managed to escape? She wondered what had happened to Blu's body, and it occurred to her that she would miss him. She would miss his cherry red rocket ship and his never-ending stash of damnable pencils. She would miss her breath when the spiders sucked it out of her.

One leapt down from the trees in front of them, and Kat struck her knife out without thinking. The spider's leg felt like flesh and bone, not exoskeleton. Its hair was not stiff and coarse as she expected, but thick and soft, conveying an invitation to pet it that sent shivers down her spine. The dog snapped at one leg while she hacked at another, keeping the beast too occupied to bite either of them, but effectively halting their advance toward the ship.

Kat could see the metallic sheen of it winking at her in the distance, mocking them with its nearness. How frustrating, she thought, to die within sight of one's freedom. She knew that many men and women had been in this situation before, just as many would continue to be after her, and she imagined that there was a gathering place in the afterlife, a bar where they could pull up a stool, share their stories, and compare war wounds. What a story she would have to tell. She looked down at the pink dog, slashed down to its red skin here and there in parts. What a good dog, looking out for her until the bitter end. What a good dog. What a shame they were going to die here.

Through the speakers came an ear-splitting squeal that suddenly deafened her. The dog howled. Kat dropped the knife, her hands flying to her ears in pain, but she noticed that the spider had shriveled up in response to the frequency as well. She pushed the dog along, away from the beast. Catherine could keep up the racket indefinitely, Kat was sure, but very soon the noise would force her to pass out. And it wasn't keeping all the spiders at bay—the pair was still being followed in droves. But they made it to the ramp of the ship, just as a spider took hold of her leg—her already bad leg—and bit down hard upon it.

Kat screamed, unable to hear her own voice above the din from the speakers. She felt the spider's many legs envelop her body, trying to pull her further down into its mouth. She kicked at its eyes with her free leg, scooting backward into the ship inch by precious inch. The dog barked madly, but while the spider lost purchase on the ramp several times, his jaws never relaxed on her leg. Kat leaned as far into the ship as she could, hefting the front of her body high enough to reach the door release. She prayed one last time, that the door would be heavy enough, that its edge would be sharp enough, and that the pain would be quick. She bit the sleeve of her suit hard and pulled the door handle down.

She was right on only the first two accounts.

Kat swam in and out of consciousness. She unzipped her suit and removed her undershirt, using it to staunch the excessive flow of blood that poured out from what used to be her leg right below the knee. On the next round of lucidity, she pulled herself into the pilot's chair and set coordinates. Any message that she might have recorded at that point would be unintelligible, so she hoped that whoever discovered her would be smart enough to figure out what to do. Neither would she be repairing the short-circuiting beacon that had led them here, to this place where a many-legged death had waited for them. Perhaps the doomed Librarian of Robinson Seven preferred it that way.

She passed out there again for a while, and woke to the sound of bodies slamming against the shell of the ship. Vengefully, she started the engines and reveled in the screams as their bodies charred and fell away.

She hallucinated a little, imagined that she saw stars before they had taken off, that the dog was somehow no longer a dog, that he could fly this ship, his ship. He stood on pink hind legs and spoke to her in words and sentences that she did not understand, but whose meaning she comprehended completely. Somehow, she made it to the chamber in the wall, lay down on the extended slab, and sealed herself inside before the world swam away from her again. She dreamt of dreaming, of being asleep on a cloud of spices. Blu was beside her, carving chunks out of the mist with his pencil and drawing hairy legs to attach to them. There was no sunlight. There was only darkness, like a mother's arms, safe and warm.

HAPPY THOUGHTS

Sorscha had never known her father's true motivation behind poisoning his children. Passion for Rasputin, Napoleon and Hitler? Paranoia-driven sense of preservation? Completely sadistic experiment? Whatever his reasons, her immunity to arsenic always made for an interesting topic of conversation at dinner parties.

She had never told her father about the hallucinations. They were her own treasures, her happy thoughts, her best friends for twenty-five years of a life that seemed a magnet for the worst kinds of abuse. She took comfort in knowing that they would always be there for her—Patches, the bear with the bow tie and plastic balloon; Crash, the monkey with the red coat; and Wind, the unicorn.

Wind. He only came to her when things were at their worst. He had come to her the night Jeff had beaten her to within an inch of her life, right before his drunken ass had run off the road and met God and a telephone pole.

Sorscha knew he would come to her tonight.

Tears ran silent rivers down her cheeks. Minerva. That redheaded bitch had finally made her cry at work, something Sorscha had sworn she would never do again in her life. Minerva was a praise-greedy pig, a passive-aggressive witch, a back-stabbing weasel, a slow poison to which Sorscha knew there was no immunity. Not even time.

Time only made it worse, as what little self-confidence she had wore away and her life sank deeper and deeper into the mire of living hell. The only reason Sorcha kept coming back was the picture behind her boss's desk. If Minerva had somehow given birth to a beautiful, intelligent child like Daisy, Sorscha was convinced that there must be something redeemable inside her. Surely.

Sorscha felt a kinship with Daisy. She knew what kind of life the child had to look forward to. Minerva's words would be Daisy's arsenic—slow and painful and never leaving any visible marks. Daisy would spend her whole life trying to make peace with this woman, trying to find love in a heart that knew no definition of the word. Once she lost that blessed innocence, Daisy would never know a life without pain.

Sorscha felt Wind's hot breath on her shoulder as a tear dripped off her chin. She turned her head into the unicorn's face and patted him, her hand slipping in the blood that slid slowly down his horn and soaked his mane.

It was a closed-casket funeral.

Sorscha moved through the black clouds of murmuring mourners until she found her, and Daisy flew into her arms without a word. Sorscha held the fragile child tightly to her. Daisy wasn't crying—already having learned the strength to resist that weakness—but her tiny limbs trembled with the weight of the world. Sorscha knew what confused emotions warred inside that little breast.

"Mama's dead," Daisy said into her shoulder.

"There, there," Sorscha whispered into the child's titian hair. "Think happy thoughts."

DIARY OF A GHOST'S MISTRESS

April 12, 1946

You left me here, you bastard. Left me in this picturesque burg on a river bend strewn with wretched Nazi refuse, left me weeping in this tower—the only part of this rotting castle that's still in one piece. Godforsaken, as Mama would say. This country, this town, this pile of crumbling rocks, me. I miss Mama. I hear her sometimes, in the back of my head. *Sit up straight. Don't overcook the chicken. Chew your food. Smell the roses. Smile into the sunshine.*

I hear you too. Telling me to be strong; telling me I'm going to be all right; telling me I'm your princess. I wake up to your voice every morning, whispering "Maddie" in my ear, and every morning I open my eyes to nothing. I know I'm depressed, and I understand that you're never coming back, but I want you to be there in that second—just for a second—so I can yell at you: Why? Why did you have to make me love you so damn much? Why did you save that old man, and then accept his gift of this decrepit piece of architecture? He gets to live—he gets to live!— in his million-year-old not-falling-down ancestral home with his family, his wife and son, his baronial pomp and circumstance.

What it is that makes living such a plus? We had a storybook life, you and I, and our happily ever after lasted as long as it took for you to get your ass blown out of the sky. Where is my family, the family you promised me, the forever we were going to create in this hamlet on the river? I am exiled here, worlds away from our apple pie world, lying in a cold bed with a flat belly, a broken heart, and half a soul.

They've made me their muse, did you know that? After the atrocities and the rape of both custom and countryside, the Mosel river folk have made me *their* princess in the tower. The Mistress of Beilstein Castle. I am the heroine of a tragic romance, a victim of fate, as they are. I have become the embodiment of this new world sprung from the old. They have set aside their history and their differences and banded together to repair this monument, in my honor. For their honor. I should be honored.

Mostly, I just miss you. And I hate myself for it.

April 15

They found buried treasure today. Hans (the only one I can remember—he's the best at pantomime translation) presented me with a filigree box this afternoon. It seemed tiny in his large hands, muscular and browned from the sun and glistening with sweat from his team having finally smashed the boulder that had blocked the path to our door. I try not to look at his face for too long. I'm pretty sure he's married, but I don't want to give the wrong impression. Once upon a time I was a no-count girl from the sticks of America; even if I spoke enough German to say so, they wouldn't believe me. To them, I am beautiful and untouchable.

These people have given me a reason to get out of bed every morning, to put lipstick on and keep the pin curls in my hair. I have a responsibility. I have a reputation to uphold as their inspiration. I cannot become a destitute harlot who pays her debts with the only currency she's got. We've seen enough cowardice and tragedy these past few years. They need strength. I need to be strong for them.

There you are again in the back of my head reminding me how strong I am. If you only knew the effort it took, empty day after empty day, to breathe the next breath.

The treasure was a music box; inside was an iron key. The key's not much to look at but the detail on the box is exquisite: painstakingly carved bullfrogs and cellophane-winged dragonflies and lilies edged in gold. The sad tune it plays was written by an infatuated composer who needed no crass words to devalue the intensity of his desire. I wish it had been a cheerful Andrews Sisters ditty I could dance to and harmonize with off-key through the echoing halls. It hurts to hold this precious gift from a man to his beloved, with sweet nothings hidden in the nooks of those exquisite details.

I'll imagine that you gave me this treasure, that frogs are my favorite animal, that lilies are my favorite flower, that this was the first song you played on your little portable Mikiphone to welcome me to our new home, and that the key opened a present you had hidden for me to find. I'll pretend it doesn't torture me to know that's all a lie.

April 16

I tried to be helpful in the kitchen, but the women shooed me away from their plucking and baking, as if my presence would spoil the milk or stop the bread from rising, as if I were incapable of making a decision more complicated than which of my three skirts to wear today (the cornflower blue one, loose now and faded; everything I own seems to have faded right along with me). Hans's crew was working on the front door this morning, the secondary crew was on the back stairs, and the women who weren't bustling about the kitchen had rounded up the children and set to work in the gardens and the grape vines in the hills beyond. Bit of a useless life, really, this being a princess. And then I remembered the key.

It took me the better part of the day to find the lock that matched the iron key. Silly me, once I found it, it made so much sense that I wondered why it hadn't occurred to me to check the belfry first. The bell had long since been "requisitioned," so there didn't seem to be any need to get to it. The door took some convincing, a bruised shoulder, and some bloody knuckles, but it finally gave way to a world forgotten by all but the spiders and birds. No bats, thankfully. I can live with this mess, but no bats.

I hauled the water and rags up myself and they let me, after wrapping me in an apron and putting what smelled like lemon juice in the water—I have no idea where the lemons came from. It stung my knuckles, but I was so excited to finally have a project I could focus on, so excited to learn that I still had the ability to be excited at all, that I didn't mind. I scrubbed until my fingers puckered and my bones ached from kneeling on the cold, hard floor. And when the water in the bucket turned darker than the stone, I tossed it out the window (Yes dear, I looked first), trekked down to the kitchens, and hauled up some more.

At dusk a young woman—she was probably about my age, but I feel so much older now—appeared. A kerchief caught up her straw-colored hair and her rough, homespun gown was long enough to cover her knees. I have no idea how long she'd been working before I noticed her. As hard as she scrubbed, the stones beneath her remained as dirty as before. After a few minutes, she noticed me back.

"My name is Danika," she said in perfect, only slightly accented English.

"My name is Maddie." It was stranger to hear my own voice than my own language. Exactly how long had I been silent as our belless tower? I did not offer my washerwoman's hand, and she was not offended. I imagine she felt some relief in being spared the disappointment of ineffective contact. We were not so different, she and I. And as I had—have—been communicating with the dead in my own way for some time now, I did not feel awkward or afraid to see her.

What I did feel was anger. Perhaps I needed to see her, behind the locked door in the belfry; perhaps she needed me to see her. But I wanted to scream through tears of rage with my rediscovered voice, to lob my filthy bucket through her insubstantial head. At some point this evening, the veil between the living and the dead parted and *you didn't step through it.*

Bastard.

April 17

I thought about ending it today. I stood on a window ledge in the belfry. The town below was so beautiful from that windy perch: rolling vine-covered hills and humble brown roofs and cobblestone streets that led down to the quiet river. Even the poisoned lands beyond seemed to shine proudly on the horizon with a glimmer of hope. It was a world shrouded in peace, and I coveted that.

The solitude makes me melancholy, and I am left alone to steep in it so long that I drown. It becomes the only place my mind goes in its waking hours. One step forward, one foot held out and one subtle shift in weight, and that peace would be mine forever. I could part the veil myself and find you on the other side. But I didn't want to.

Did that make me brave? Or had I chosen the coward's path?

Thing is, crazy as it may sound, I don't want my life to end. But I don't want to simmer in the sadness anymore. I desperately want my mind to be occupied with any subject but you.

"If you're going to jump, you should take off your clothes first." Danika's voice was an almost imperceptible soft echo in my skull—I felt what she said more than heard it. On some level, I suppose I was just talking to myself.

"Why?" I needed the conversation more than the answer.

"It would be a shame to waste such a lovely skirt. The people have little enough as it is. I think Leisle's about your size. She'd appreciate it."

(I only know a handful of names, but if memory serves, Leisle is the woman in charge of the kitchen who is built like a tree stump with ham hocks for arms.) I smiled and coughed, as laughing was still too foreign. She had a concerned expression on her translucent face, so I stepped down off the sill to ease her mind. "Is that what you did?"

Danika moved to the far end of the room—not so far, as the belfry was relatively small, but the stalwart army of cobwebs there had not yet met the wrath of my rag. She moved with the glide and hesitation of paper caught in a cold wind, then stopped and stared ahead at what I finally realized was a dark door. Careful to leave my incorporeal roommate a wide berth, I pulled on the door. My sore muscles screamed before the swollen wood finally gave way. Inside was a dress, once white, a more romantic version of something I had worn in days of music and skin and all the laughter I've lost.

That she had removed the gown before she jumped meant she treasured a love, consciously kept it apart from the horrible thing she had been about to do. I looked through her again. The horrible thing she had done.

"Promise me," she said, and took my breath with the passion in her voice, "promise me that when the frog comes to you with the key that you will tell no one."

And whom would I tell? So I said, "I promise."

"The owner of this castle was a robber baron." Her voice reverberated between my ears, sometimes thick with accent, sometimes singing, sometimes in a language I could not comprehend if I concentrated too hard upon the words. "He was obsessed with hoarding the treasures he had stolen, hiding them so well that legends grew around him. When he died, the location of the treasure died with him. It was said that a giant toad guarded the castle, with fiery eyes and teeth, ready to devour anyone who sought the treasure."

Danika's body faded in and out with the telling, but her voice remained strong. I tried to focus on the window beyond her, on the blue sky and errant clouds. "Ranulf and I were traveling on foot from Kaiserslautern, following the ringing of tower bell, when the frog came to me." Her beloved's name was a sweet she held under her tongue, though the name of her hometown left a bitter taste on mine. You made your mark on history there, and perished. And much as I might owe him, I do not like to think about the selfless baron from Kaiserslautern, who gave you this cursed place.

"Ranulf was born in the woods but I have never been a good walker; I fell behind on the path. The Robber Baron appeared as a giant frog with a golden crown, and offered me the golden key in his mouth. He told me of the treasure in this castle, his treasure, and said that I might have my pick of his hoard."

"On one condition," I guessed.

"I held that key and promised him that I would tell no one. I was so confident, so arrogant. When I caught back up to my beloved, the secret burned inside my breast. The bell had stopped ringing, and Ranulf wondered if perhaps we would not be welcome, if perhaps we should pass it by until we reached the next town. I did not mean to tell him; I merely hinted that we needed—that I needed…" Her voice fell away, and when it continued again, her lips were not moving. "When we reached the castle, the key was gone."

She stared with me through the same casement at the same

idyllic scene below. I wondered if what she saw there were the same hills and the same clouds and the same swans flying past. "Ranulf commended me for my storytelling, and moved on as if nothing had changed. But I had changed. The baron had planted the seed of his obsession inside me, and I lusted after a treasure I had never seen. And never will."

"Never?" Surely even Beilstein Castle could not keep secrets from the spirits who walked through its walls.

"I ignored my dreams, hid my obsession until the day we were to be married." She cast a glance over her shoulder at the dress; she had remembered again to move her lips to match the words in my head, but they were still out of sync. "I could not marry Ranulf; he deserved a partner whose soul was not consumed by other desires. I was no longer that woman. I burned to seek the treasure that had eluded me. So I ran. I don't know how long. I ran here." She looked down at her feet, now dirty and bare, laced with angry lines of blood.

"There was only one way to guarantee that the treasure would reveal itself to me." She turned away from the window, her eyes the green-gray of the river below. "He wept when they carried my broken body from the stones. He stayed until I was buried. Then he left, and I could not follow. I like to think that he lived a full life, a good life, and that he did not dwell on the cursed woman who did not love him enough to stay by his side."

Perhaps I was seeing a ghost. Perhaps it was black magic. Perhaps I had gone insane. Perhaps I had jumped out of the window and my body lay broken on the stones. Who would weep for me? Who would stay with my body and see me laid to rest?

If I was imagining all of this then it was a story I was telling myself, one I needed more than wanted to hear. She smiled a half smile then, as if she knew my thoughts, and my suspicions grew.

"Do you know where the treasure is?" I asked her.

"Yes," she said, though it might have been the wind stirring the cobwebs. "It is surrounded by the only walls in this castle I cannot walk through."

*May 1 (***though it might be tomorrow already***)*

The fiery toad from hell finally approached me tonight. I've made an effort over these past few weeks to open up, to show these people how much I appreciate their efforts, to make them see how productive they are when united. Within them lies the seed of what Germany once was—it would be nice if it could be that way again everywhere.

You'd be proud of me. I've even learned a few words. Enough to get me smiled at, but not quite enough to be helpful if I fall in the river, so I do my best to tread lightly around the Mosel ferry.

Hans and his wife—I keep wanting to call her Gretel, but I think it's Gerta—took me across the river to a wine tasting. Now I know why they spit. The room's still spinning a little, but it's not like you care what my handwriting looks like anyway.

Why is it that no matter how snug your shoes are, things still manage to sneak in? Maybe pebbles are ghosts that can walk through shoe leather. No one noticed my absence for all that they were singing up a storm. I've missed singing.

By the time I had fixed myself up again, I was alone on the path. Cold and alone and the moon made strange shadows. I wished you were with me then, but if you had, he never would have come. I needed to be there. I needed to be scared. And I needed to be without you.

I thought he was a stone at first, a large, lumpy stone that some clever boy had thought to light on fire to mark the path. But I wasn't seeing double; the twin fire was eyes, and the mouth that opened below them was deep and dark and wide and lined with sharp teeth and I could imagine it opening up deeper and darker and wider enough to swallow the whole world. Starting with me. And from that deep and dark and wide mouth dropped a golden key, the size of my hand.

Princesses are not meant to pick up slimy, spit-covered things from an animal's mouth, especially if that animal is a scary ghost-demon from fiery hell and wearing a crown of smoldering napalm. But I knew this part of the story, knew what I had to. Intense cold or heat or acid spit burned my palm, but I held on to that key. Finally, my sad little life had a *purpose*.

I wondered—well, I wondered if I had scarred my hand for life and would ever be able to use it again, but I also wondered if I'd be able to get away without having to swear that vow of silence. He did finally speak, the same way that Danika "spoke" to me, not from the lips, but straight into my head, an echo in my brain. Only this hurt. Pain wept from my ears and I tried to cover them with my fists.

TELL NO ONE.

I passed out right there on the path. (Don't worry, I'm okay.) When woke up, the toad was gone. My palm was not burned…nor was it empty. I have been holding that key so tightly now that my fingers have gone numb, but I refuse to let it go. I plan to hold it in my sleep tonight, and hopefully by tomorrow I will have thought of a way to tell Danika without actually *telling* her.

May 2

It's not quite dawn, which is good. I know exactly what to do. I am going to march straight up to the belfry and put on Danika's dress. She's a little taller than me, but I'm thinner, so as long as it stays in one piece, it will do the job. I'll just toss it on over my chemise—if I hide the key in my garter she'll never see it.

She'll follow me. I'm hoping she'll be smart enough to figure it out by the time we get to the main hall, so she can lead me where I need to go. I will not utter a word to anyone I pass. Since that's not out of the ordinary for me anyway, it should be easy peasy japanesey.

I am glad I can tell you, though. Funny, isn't it, how things work out. If you had been here I would have lost this key in a heartbeat, and you would have lost me to obsession instead of the other way around. I never needed to keep secrets from you, but there are so many things I wish I could have said. I would have told you I loved you a thousand more times. I would have thanked you for saving me from my boring life and bringing me here to this place where I can be useful, to the ghost and this town being reborn before my eyes. I would have told you how lucky I was—I am—to have had you in my life for what little bit of time the universe allowed. I would have said goodbye.

Goodbye, my love. I have a dress to wear and a ghost to put to rest and a golden key in my fist now damp with sweat and trembling with anticipation. I don't care about any stupid treasure. I'm doing this for Danika. I almost hope it doesn't work. I will miss having someone to talk to. Wish me luck!

May 3

You'll have to forgive my handwriting again—apparently it's just as terrible when I'm brimming with happiness as it is after a wine tasting and a visit from fiery hell.

The dress worked, though it was moldy and full of dust and I was worried as I flew down the stairs and hallways that it might crumble to pieces and leave me in my underwear. I ran out of the belfry toward the main hall, streaming dark hair and bare white feet beneath that ancient wedding dress. This morning, in the false-light of dawn, *I* was the ghost of Beilstein Castle. I was a dead woman ready to return to the land of the living. Finally.

Hans and his crew had fixed the front door but not the frame around it, and a cold wind whipped through my hair, tossing the skirt of the dress, enveloping me in a cloud of dust. The cloud resolved itself into Danika's face and she led me down, down, down into the basement, into the wine cellar. A handful of yellow, caged light bulbs hung in rows from the ceiling and like the moon in the woods threw strange shadows before us, and possibly after us too, but I did not look back.

Deep in the maze of half-empty racks was a wall like every other wall, only not lined with casks. Danika stopped, and hovered behind me. I leaned down and brushed the layers of dirt off the wall, uncovering the frog etched there and the keyhole in the center of its deep, dark mouth. Triumphant, I hefted the crumbling skirts, pulled the golden key out of my garter, and shoved it in.

It took what seemed like forever for the hidden gears and pulleys to remember their duties and open the secret door. It took another forever for my eyes to adjust to the dark inside, once illuminated by what little incandescence the cellar had to offer. I fantasized about what the treasure trove of a robber baron might hold. What finally met the light before me was more beautiful than the piles of gold and jewels I had imagined: rows and rows of paintings, books, and portraits, generations of a family locked in time, untouched by war. There was history here that I knew would be more important to this town—my town—than all the riches in the world. These people had been the baron's most precious treasure, and now they were mine. I fell to my knees before them, no longer mindful of splitting seams or rending fabric, and would have wept if not for the wonder of it all.

"Baroness?" His voice was richer than the darkest wine. I was afraid to look up from my heap in the shadows on the cold stone floor; I did not want the baron to gaze upon me with his fiery eyes, to force me to choose only one item from this precious inventory. But I could not resist; I turned my face into the light and was blinded.

The man turned off the flashlight. "Baroness?" he repeated, then proceeded to spew a stream of rapid-fire German that I had no hope of understanding. His deep voice followed every move his lips made, and did not bleed in my ears. He was not the ghost of the robber baron. I heard him say "Kaiserslautern," but he was far too young to be the magnanimous eccentric who paid you for his life with this lovely pile of rocks.

He must have noticed that I could not understand him, because his monologue slowly dwindled to nothing. Instead of continuing on, he extended his hand to help me off the floor. I took it, sliding my icy fingers into his warm ones, and we turned our heads toward the gasp at the door.

I do not know if he saw Danika there, weeping invisible tears. What a picture we must have made, surrounded by the fiery toad's priceless treasure, me on the floor in her gown, the baron's son taking my hand. In another life we might have been Danika and Ranulf, and that was enough. She faded then, forever, and my bruised heart broke into pieces at her loss. I did not know if I possessed the strength to ever stand again.

The baron's son did not release my hand. "*Ich habe eine glocke,*" he said slowly. My brow furrowed. He had *what?* He closed his eyes, concentrated a moment, and then said in halting English, "I have…brought you…a bell."

My laugh echoed loud in the hidden chamber, rusty but no longer forgotten. My heart, my castle, would be whole again. I stood, and let him lead me back into the light.

His name is Karl. You would like him.

RED LANTERN

"If you'd tilt your head ever so slightly down, Mrs. Crunchmueller…" Jack turned the camera's lens away from the autumn dusk outside his apartment window.

"How many times do I have to tell you, Jack? Call me Molly."

"Of course. Molly." Jack snapped a picture. It didn't matter what he called her. She was Married-Money-Prada-and-Vuitton-Food-on-the-Table-Paying-Customer. She was the upper crust level to which he had sunk, whoring himself out by painting portraits to survive while the muse eluded him.

"My husband was so happy with the piece you did for his office."

"As you said before. I'm honored." Touched, Jack thought. Thrilled. Ecstatic. I'll clean the sheets, love; just leave your money on the table.

Molly's eye caught the satin-covered canvas in the corner and she perked up. Intrigue erased years from her face. She perched on the edge of the sofa as the blushing bride, the nervous debutante. "Is that your next?"

"Yes." He took the photos at a rapid-fire pace, soaking up the light and fairy dust that emanated from her.

"Do you think I might—?" She was a child peering into the window of a candy shop.

"No," he said over the machine gun of the shutter. "Sorry. Bad luck. You understand."

"Of course." Her face fell. As quickly as it had come, the magic was gone. Jack lowered the camera, unsure if he should be disappointed that the moment had passed or happy that she could leave now. She pushed her silver hair behind her ear and Jack caught a fleeting glimpse of unevenness in her skin. Facelift.

As innocent as it had seemed, the habitual gesture lost something in the juxtaposition. He wondered if her daughter had inherited the same tendency. Or her granddaughter. He fiddled with the camera, the unnecessary impression of business while she scrawled out round numbers on her checkbook with her diamond-studded pen. The crisp tear was the click of another lock on his personal hell. So much weight on his soul for such a small scrap of paper.

"I'll have the preliminary sketch done next week, if you'd like to come by."

"Thank you, Mr. Brown," teased Molly.

Jack forced a grin onto his face. "A pleasure as always, Mrs…Molly."

She nodded, glancing once more to the corner of the room before walking out the door. Jack set the camera on the table and stood before the shrouded canvas, trying to see it through her eyes. Beneath that satin was the next great work from one of the area's most promising up-and-coming artists. Had he given her half a chance, Molly would have written him a check for that as well, sight unseen. After selling out the entirety of his first art show, the local mavens were overly anxious to get their hands on his next masterpiece/work-in-progress/grocery list.

He should have mentioned it. He should have sold it to her. He should have handed it over for whatever cash she had on her. But some small shred of dignity—all that remained of the true artist buried deep within him—wouldn't allow it. He reached out and slowly pulled the satin from the easel, forcing himself to remember what was still there.

The empty canvas stared back at him.

Ashamed, Jack's gaze slipped to the floor. A black cat wound its way around the legs of the easel and rubbed its whiskers lazily against the wood. A galaxy of stars decorated the emerald green collar around its neck.

"*No.* No, no, no." Jack scooped up the cat, stomped to the front of his apartment and threw open the door.

The Downtown Harvest Festival had exploded in the corridor.

An overwhelming odor of cinnamon and nutmeg assailed his senses. Assorted gourds and squash were arranged in baskets and stacked in piles. Silk leaves every color of autumn's rainbow decorated the walls and door moldings. He tripped over a pile of sticks and rocks, catching himself painfully on the garland-wrapped banister. He looked closer to examine what exactly had poked into his now glitter-covered and apple-scented palm. Miniature pumpkins and wicked cornucopias winked back at him.

The cat dug its claws into his arm.

A broom decorated with a star-spangled black ribbon hung on the wide-open door beside a sign that said, "Happy Halloween, Whatever You Are." Beside the door was an empty pedestal about four feet high. Backing through the door, arms laden with a huge ceramic carved pumpkin, was the black-haired, green-eyed witch. She carefully navigated the threshold and turned, her eyes alight upon seeing him. "Why, Baa-sil," she mocked in an English accent. "How good to see you. All wrapped up for the day?"

Jack bristled. He hated Cassie. She had started calling him "Baa-sil" on his birthday, directly after gifting him with a copy of The Picture of Dorian Gray. Not that Jack would have minded being referred to as Basil Hallward, Dorian's portrait artist, but she always said it in that long, drawn out accent and then giggled, tickled with herself.

"Cassandra," he said sternly, "your cat was in my apartment again."

Cassie hefted the enormous pumpkin onto the pedestal, pulling the ends of her curly hair from underneath it and wrapping them behind her head. The structure was almost as tall as she was.

"Reginald Mothcatcher, what did I tell you? You know Baa-sil doesn't like to be interrupted while he's working." Cassie mercifully extracted its claws from Jack's flesh. "How do you suppose he does it?" she asked him.

"I don't care how the little Houdini does it," Jack scolded. "But I really wish he'd stop. Can't you put him in a kennel or something?"

Cassie pouted and cuddled the cat under her chin. "He doesn't mean that, my iddy-sweetkins," she said to the cat. "We all love you, yes we do." She dropped the cat inside the doorway. Reginald looked up as Cassie pulled the door closed; Jack could have sworn the feline felon actually smiled at him. Spoiled brat.

"Sorry about that, Jack." She laughed. "Hah! Jack!" She pointed to the grinning pumpkin on the pedestal.

"Is all of this really necessary?" Jack asked futilely. "I am well aware of how much you and your little Wiccan friends love the season, but all this…"

"Halloween's *tomorrow*," she said. "You're the only other one who lives on this floor. We're at the top, Jack, and you rarely ever leave the house. So no one even walks by here unless they're visiting me. Which they will be, tomorrow, for my party. If you're nice, I'll invite you."

"My clients," Jack reminded her.

"Molly said it was charming," said Cassie. "And Mr. Rodgers said he didn't care as long as I didn't use any candles this time."

Jack closed his lids and rolled his eyes so far back in his head he thought he might need surgery to replace them. The day their septuagenarian landlord stood his ground on anything would be the day the Four Horsemen galloped through the streets of town.

Cassie retrieved two plastic glo-sticks from the breast pocket of her overalls. "Do you know the story of the other Jack?"

"No," Jack sighed. "But I'm sure you're going to tell me."

"It's actually kind of sad," she said. "That Jack, he was one clever guy. Caused all kinds of mischief. One day he even caught the Devil up a tree and trapped him there." She bent one stick and then the other, until they cracked and bled their fluorescent blood. "The Devil got away eventually, of course. But when Jack died, he wasn't allowed into Heaven because of his mischievous ways, and the Devil still held a grudge, so he wouldn't let him into Hell." She shook the sticks vigorously. "So he was left to forever wander the in-between world, with only a lantern to guide him." She removed a partially-burned white candle from the pumpkin and replaced it with the sticks. The green glow poured from its eyes, nose, and mouth, turning it sinister. "And there you have it. Jack O'Lantern."

"Fascinating," Jack said, running a hand through his hair. "Look, I'm just gonna go—"

Cassie thrust the slightly-warped candle at him. "Take this. There's a full moon tonight. A blue moon. October's the Blood Moon too. So I guess that makes this a Blueblood Moon, huh?" Her tinkling laugher echoed down the stairwell. "Which totally explains Molly Crunchmueller."

"Riiight," Jack said, backing up a pace.

Cassie stepped forward, still holding the candle out to him. "Seriously, Jack. It's Devil's Night, and you never know what evil is lurking about. White is for protection. Just take it, okay? Humor me."

Anything to shut her up. "Thanks," he said without feeling.

"Good night, Jack."

He couldn't get through the door fast enough. Once inside, he remembered why he'd left. The blank canvas screamed at him from the opposite end of the room. The moonlight illuminated the stark rectangle like a beacon. He couldn't summon the energy to lift the satin and hide it again. He would leave it, glaring, proving to the world that he was a dried-up failure. He sank to his knees before it. He squeezed colors onto his palette reflecting the spectrum of his frustration—reds only—a rainbow of anger from violet crimson to burnt sienna. Maybe if he just picked up a brush at random and went through the motions, his body would remember that it contained a genius.

He held the paint-covered bristles an inch from the canvas until his arm cramped.

Hopeless.

He was hopeless. It had been too long. There was nothing left in him. His life had no purpose. Artists were meant to create. One who could not was worth less than nothing, both to the world and to himself. A tear slid down his cheek and dropped onto his palette. Its mate landed on the blade of his canvas knife, glinting in the blue moon's light.

So this was what it had come to.

Numb, Jack pressed the knife to the inside of his wrist. The final sacrifice. He winced and then cried out as the blade pierced the delicate skin. It was a small cut, shallow, but the deepest he could force himself to make. He couldn't even kill himself properly. Blood slipped down his arm and dripped into the paint.

And suddenly he knew.

The floodgates in Jack's mind burst opened. He knew what he had to do. He was an artist without a muse. So he would paint one.

The blood-and-crimson brush touched the canvas and immediately swooped down the curve of her jaw. It played along the graceful lines of her neck. It caressed the slope of her nose. It blew wind through her hair, the hundreds and hundreds of long, streaming red locks. He painted frantically, paying no heed to the blood that dripped slowly onto his palette and the floor below. There was nothing else but her. Her lips were a gift from Venus herself, full and inviting. The curve of her shoulder lifted wantonly. Her eyes—for he painted those last—stared out from the frame all-knowing, piercing him to his very soul.

Jack fell back, every muscle drained of energy. His knees were on fire. The room was in darkness now, the moon having passed over quite some time ago. He had no idea where she had come from, but there she was: The Red Woman. His muse, his essence, his whole reason for being. She would give him his gift back, and he would give her everything left of himself in return.

Jack stared at her, his body refusing to do little more. That he could give such life to such simple lines, that he could create such passion. *This* was what they were talking about, he thought to himself. *This* is the genius I was. He tossed the brush back on to the palette and pulled his aching bones off the floor. He would clean up tomorrow. Hell, even if he had to buy all new supplies it would be worth it. She was worth it. She was worth everything.

Jack backed out of the room, his eyes never leaving her. He brushed his teeth and changed, peeking out the bathroom or the bedroom doorway every few moments to make sure he had not dreamed her. He pushed his bed to the middle of the room and slept with his head at the footboard so that when he opened his eyes he could see her the moment he awoke. He would have brought her into the room with him had he not been deathly afraid of marring her still-wet paint. He sighed and looked up at the ceiling. He smiled, his heart singing, and closed his eyes.

He couldn't sleep.

Who could blame him? He looked at her again, his heart on canvas. He closed his eyes and the outline of her shone beneath his eyelids. His obsession with her doubled every minute. She haunted him silently from across the room. He tossed and turned. He almost wished that he had not painted her, or that he had done so after a good night's rest. Catching himself, he took the thought back immediately. She was there, she was in his life, she *was* his life, and he was never letting go. He tossed some more.

When dawn finally broke through his window, he gave in and got up. Scratching and yawning, he shuffled into the kitchen and poured himself a bowl of cereal. He took it over to the couch and sat down to have breakfast with his Red Woman.

He still felt a surge in his chest every time he looked at her. She consumed him. She burned him. She blazed light from every corner. He traced each line of her with his eyes again, trying to remember exactly how it had felt when he had painted her, reliving the memory second by second.

By the time he thought to take a bite of his cereal, it was inedible.

Jack set the bowl on the table. It didn't matter. He could live off the love he had for the Red Woman. He could live off her inspiration. He filled another palette with color and went to work.

But he wasn't inspired. At least, he wasn't inspired to do anything else. Jack stood before another blank canvas and could not paint. His head was filled with only her.

Perhaps it was too soon. He was pushing it. He should take the time to revel in his perfect masterpiece before moving on. He sat before her again, the end of each nerve ablaze with energy, filled with passion.

He wanted her.

The thought struck him like a bolt of lightning. Ridiculous. She was a painting; she wasn't real. Sure, his talent had poured a soul into her that flooded the world with its brilliance, but she was no substitute for the flesh and blood thing.

Jack smiled. He imagined what the Red Woman would be like if she were flesh and blood. Her hair would be shiny and soft. Her skin would be softer. When he breathed in the nape of her neck, she would smell like copper and strawberries. Her laugh would be low and sultry. Every move, every gesture would be the epitome of grace. And when they made love, her red eyes would sparkle.

Jack shook it off.

Ridiculous.

Morning wandered into afternoon.

He walked into the bedroom and perched on the edge of the bed, rummaging through his dresser for a clean shirt. His head pounded. He closed his weary eyes for a moment.

She was there. She walked up to the bed and silently straddled him. Her arms wrapped around his neck and she licked along the edge of his stubble-covered jaw. He could feel her hair spilling down his back, the weight of her in his lap. He opened his eyes.

Nothing.

Jack fell back onto the bed, every inch of him aching for her. He was going crazy. The lack of sleep was making him delirious. He grabbed a shirt at random, pulled it on and headed to the bathroom. He caught a glimpse of himself in the mirror on the way to the toilet. Bloodshot eyes stared back at him above dark, sunken circles and unshaven scruff. He had put his shirt on inside out and backwards. Great.

Wait a minute…

He backed up.

Jack leaned closer to the mirror. Under the scruff down one

side of his jaw was a long line of red paint.

Impossible. Utterly impossible. He had just missed it last night when he was brushing his teeth. It had happened while he was painting. He just hadn't noticed. But it hadn't happened then, and Jack knew it. He knew it because every bit of the paint he had used last night had ended up on the canvas. He knew it because there had been nothing to clean up this morning but some crusty brushes and a bit of dried blood on the floor. He knew it because he knew what wet paint felt like, and at no time last night had a brush ever come close to his face.

No. Impossible. He shoved the thought out of his mind and went to relieve himself.

But what if it wasn't impossible? What if, by some amazing circumstance, such strange magic existed? What if someone believed in something so much it came true?

Jack rushed back out to the living room and looked at the painting again.

He didn't just want the Red Woman. He *needed* her with every fiber of his being. There had to be a way to make her real, to call her to him in the flesh. But what sort of thing did a body have to do to make magic that powerful happen?

Magic.

Jack smacked himself in the forehead. Ask the witch.

He tore himself away from the painting long enough to throw on a pair of jeans before dashing out the door.

A few of Cassie's guests had arrived and were scattered about the landing. A cowboy in a ten-gallon hat aimed a suction dart at the hindquarters of a woman in a catsuit arranging canapés and fired.

"Nice shootin', Dex!" twin devils cheered.

Jack made his way past a hippie and a mountie who were deep in conversation with a dark-haired gypsy. Cassie's living room was empty save for a man on the couch dressed like a monkey, complete with Persian robes and fez. The monkey on his shoulder wore jeans and a dark gray shirt. The man was hunched over a bowl of nuts, picking out the cashews and every so often tossing one to his companion.

"Where's Cassie?" Jack asked desperately.

The man motioned over his shoulder with his thumb. The monkey did the same.

"Thanks." Jack crossed the room and knocked impatiently on the bedroom door.

"Come in." Cassie stood before him, resplendent in white. Her empire-waist gown was covered in glitter, complementing the pair of very large iridescent gauze wings. Her raven curls spilled down her back in contrast. She looked up and caught his reflection in the mirror. "Oh my God, Jack. What's wrong?"

"I need your help."

"Sure. Of course. Anything," she said. "You look like death warmed over. Are you okay?"

"Yes. No." He nodded and shook his head in turn. "Cassie, I need to ask you something. How do you make magic?"

Cassie raised an eyebrow. "What?"

"You're a witch. How do you make magic? I need to know."

Cassie narrowed her eyes at him. "I don't know what you're playing at, but I have a party to get to. So if you'll excuse me..."

She tried to brush past him but he grabbed her. The silver ivy circlet around her upper arm dug into his palm. "I'm serious, Cassie. You need candles, right? What else?"

Cassie lifted her star-tipped wand and pinned him back with it. "Look here, Jack. You're either making fun of me, or you're not. If you're making fun of me, fine, great. I can take it, but let's do it another time." She pressed down harder, and he backed into the wall. The constellations of rhinestones at her temples intensified the fire in her eyes. "If you're *not* making fun of me, then you're messing with something that should not be messed with. Not by you, and not tonight of all nights. Go home, Jack. Get some sleep. If you wake up later, come back to the party."

Speechless, Jack left her room. The man and the monkey were gone. On the couch were now a princess and a samurai cat locked in a passionate embrace, kissing like they had lived their entire lives across the world from each other and were making up for lost time. Jack ached with envy. He wanted some of that passion, that feeling of completion. He needed the Red Woman. She was not just the other half of his soul, she *was* his soul. He didn't know how he had lived without her until now. He wasn't sure how he could go on living.

How hard could it be, right? He'd figure it out, with or without the witch's help.

He made his way back through the crowd, declining the hors d'oeuvres offered by the catwoman. By the time he was back inside the simple silent world of his apartment, he had decided on a couple of things he could try. He rummaged in the kitchen until he found a lighter, and then lit the candle Cassie had forced upon him. He turned the painting so that the full moon once again filled the canvas, glorifying his love. If she had been beautiful before, she was magnificent now.

Jack knelt on the floor and held the candle before him. Cassie had said that white candles were for protection. It should be enough to keep him safe from any boogymonsters he might summon.

The Red Woman leveled him with her eyes. Oh, who was he kidding. If she inspired him in the flesh half as much as she inspired him without it, he would be a fool not to pull her into his world no matter what the consequences.

Muted laughter filtered through his door, but he ignored it. He closed his eyes and stilled his breathing. He thought of magic, of faith and conviction. He filled himself with it. He felt the moonlight caressing his skin. Slowly, he raised his arms.

"Abracadabra!"

He opened his eyes.

The Red Woman mocked him from the canvas.

Jack deflated. That's it, boy, he told himself. You've officially gone off the deep end. What on earth did he think he was going to accomplish? Magic didn't really exist.

But there was magic in what he felt for the Red Woman. There had been magic in her creation. There was magic in her inspiration. There was magic all around her. A life without that wasn't worth living.

The thought dragged a memory up to the surface. He set the candle down beside him, the melted wax guttering the flame. Grabbing the canvas knife once again, he pierced the tip of his finger. Blood welled up almost instantly. With it he lovingly traced the line of the Red Woman's lips. In fairy tales, the kiss of true love was the most powerful magic of all. What did he have to lose? He leaned forward and pressed his lips to hers.

He felt like a complete idiot. He was so desperate. It wasn't going to work. His heart cried out one last time.

A red painted hand reached out from the canvas and tangled its fingers in his hair.

Jack threw himself into the kiss, wanting to cry out in disbelief and ecstasy but not willing to break contact. He reached into the canvas and wrapped his arms around his Red Woman. Tears of happiness fell from his eyes. He pulled at her. She pulled back. The thought that she might have wanted him as much as he wanted her had never even crossed his mind; now it dizzied him. They pressed into each other desperately, the lines blurring where one body stopped and the other began. He ran his hands down her hair, his hair. He felt the slippery-paint smoothness of her skin, his skin. His hand drifted down her belly, his belly. And to the emptiness below that…

Jack's eyes snapped open in fear and his stomach instantly rolled over. The world had turned itself inside out. The body he had now was not his own. It was her body, the Red Woman's body. It took him a minute to realize that he was now looking into his apartment from the canvas.

His own body looked back at him and winked.

There was a soft knock on the door, and Other Jack turned to answer it. Cassie stood there, a vision in white, the lights of the party illuminating her translucent wings. The ribbons of her magic wand trailed to the ground. She must have known he needed help.

She was his angel of mercy, come to rescue him. He had never seen anything so beautiful before in his life.

"Hey," she said softly to Other Jack. "Look, I just wanted to apologize for what I said before."

"It's okay," Other Jack said. "I just… I haven't been able to paint. I'm little overtired." He smiled at her. "And I guess a little desperate."

What the hell? Was the demon body snatcher *hitting* on Cassie? Jack tried to yell a warning at her from the painting, but it was no use.

"I've been worried about you, Jack."

"Been worried about myself too, lately." Other Jack ran a hand through his hair.

No! Jack screamed without words at the familiar gesture. You can't do that! That's something *I* do! He tried to fill his soul with that same energy as before and direct it towards Cassie. Look at me, Cassie, he pleaded. Look at me. *Look at me.*

Cassie turned her head. "But you *have* been painting." She crouched down in front of the canvas. "She's beautiful."

"You think so?" asked Other Jack.

"She is a little…intense," Cassie said. "What were you going for?"

Other Jack sighed. "Someone more like you, actually."

Oh give me a *break*, Jack groaned. Do you honestly think she's going to fall for—?

Cassie blushed. "That's sweet, Jack. You know all you had to do was ask." She took his hand in hers. "Come on. Come to my party. Please?"

Other Jack looked down at his paint-stained jeans, his inside-out shirt. "Give me a sec, okay?"

Cassie laughed. "Okay." A woman in camouflage walked past the apartment, accompanied by a six-foot tall squirrel. Jack watched as his raven-haired salvation joined them and closed the door behind her.

Other Jack walked over to the palette and emptied an entire tube of paint on it. Blue or black, Jack couldn't tell. Other Jack picked up a stiff wide brush and coated it liberally. He paused with the bristles an inch away from the canvas.

"Sorry 'bout this, Jack," Other Jack said. His voice was different now, his accent thick. "Old Scratch's rules: an eye for an eye, a life for a life. A man's gotta do, you know?" He rested the bristles on the canvas. "Best o'luck, mate."

Jack thought back on his life as the paint erased his apartment bit by bit. So many things he had wanted to do, so many things he would have done differently. Thoughts and deeds and sounds and smells…in a moment there would be only blackness, the empty nothingness of the Devil's in-between world.

But he did have something, something he hadn't realized until now. It sat in his hand, small, lumpy, and waxy.

Cassie's white candle sputtered to life, his sole companion in a darkness where light cast no shadow.

DEATHDAY

You gave to me the breath of life
The day I started dying
And with your palm you wiped away
The tears I started crying
Through your breast flowed to me
All your sorrow, love and pain
The tribulations of your life
Drowned me in their rain
And cried I so to learn it all
To see it in my mind
The path I had been set to walk
The hands the ropes would bind
I felt a strong emotion
That I later named as fear
To see the other end so far
As this end starts right here
But 'fore I learned that footstep
To start me on my way
Before I walked the tightrope
I heard the brilliance say

You have this dagger in your hand
A gift from me to you
And as you walk your path of life
There's something you should do
Cut away the iron chains
Should temptation bind you
Cut a way into the fog
Should vengeance ever find you
Let it make your decisions
Should doubt dare ask you why
And thrust it hard and deeply
Should the devil pass you by

As if his name did call him
The devil did appear
And with his visage vanished
All my petty thoughts of fear
I stared at his perfection
The half which made me whole
That perfect imperfection
That called him to my soul
He was this place, this darkness
This world that he had made
And I stood here, his mirror
He looked and was afraid
Ignoring the presence at my side
That brilliance from above
He saw in me his depth of hatred

Depth of anger, depth of love

He knew that I could never love him

Or fall prey to any lie

For he knew I'd never leave him

Not to live is not to die

Sadly he fell to his knees

And pity drew me near

Painfully he took my hand

And whispered in my ear

I see this dagger in your hand

The gift from Him to you

Before you walk your path of life

There's something you must do

Kill me swift and surely

If you ever want to live

The sacrifice is mine alone

Mine alone to give

I felt the dagger smooth and cold

I could not laugh, I could not cry

I felt the brilliance grow in triumph

But I could not let him die

The deed was mine to do and so

The sacrifice his never

The choice was mine to live and love

Or be with him forever

For I could never learn to love

If I chose not my life

I'd be emotionless, immortal

If I chose not the knife
But should I learn to live and love
I'd also learn to doubt him
And when time came for me to die
I'd do it so without him
The brilliance there lit up the world
To see the darkness small and weak
The false hope grew infinite
When my tear fell from his cheek

I raised the dagger above my head
One of us would leave here dead
I raised the dagger above my head
And thrust it in my heart instead

From that non-existent place
I heard the brilliance crying
From that non-existent place
I heard my darkness sighing
My soul fused with the silver blade
And I became that sword of truth
The moment before my mother
Introduced me to my youth

I thank you for this magic gift
That only you could give
I thank you for the gambling dare
You challenged me to live

But still she's always searching
Somewhere deep inside me
For that perfect imperfection
Hers are the ropes that tied me
She's searching for her other half
Eternally she's crying
For that sacrifice she made
The day she started dying

Confessions of the Ex-Future-Mrs. X

He was one in a million.

No, wait—that's not right. That's too many. Probably closer to the truth to say one in a billion, but it's still hard for me to believe that five other people on this planet could be that amazing. That unique. That happy. That loved. That insane.

How did we meet? I thought everybody knew that story. The short version: through a mutual friend, in a café halfway across the world. God, that feels like lifetimes ago, back before he was the man we'll call "Xavier Xanadu." Before the purple suits and the Albert Einstein-do. Before he was The Candy Man—if anyone can remember such a time—he was just a man, sitting at a table, sipping tea, and dreaming through rose-colored glasses.

But there was still magic. There was always magic.

To answer the question you're not asking: no. It wasn't love at first sight. I had a boatload of my own troubles in the World of Me, and had it been left to my devices there never would have been anything between us beyond that meeting. But he wore me down, infecting me with that contagious enthusiasm. He made me laugh like I hadn't laughed in ages. You know, that kind of addictive, honest belly-laugh that goes on forever and makes your stomach cramp and brings tears to your eyes. The first time I had cried in ages too. Like a child. He made me laugh like I had when I was a child, when the world was innocent and wonderful.

But that was his gift.

How long were we together? More than three years. Less than five. I don't know exactly. I've never really wanted to add up everything I stole from him, and that time was definitely part of it. I know, I know…they say you can't steal something that's given freely, but they're wrong. You can. You can take it, knowing that you're taking it, and knowing that you won't, can't, give any of it back.

Those years of "us" were really all about me, and he made it that way. He gave me things I needed and things I wanted, and things it hadn't even occurred to me to need or want. He knew I had a sweet tooth and he encouraged that.

He opened the door, and I jumped through it.

He had a friend—back when he was called such by a mere handful and not the whole world—who got me a job as a reviewer. A food critic, a job that became more and more specific until I secured the cake job (excuse the pun) of reviewing only dessert shops and bakeries. I bathed in a chocolate-drizzled dream topped with whipped cream and raspberries.

Xavier saw my reaction to the sweet side of life, so he took it a step further. He made new berries. He created a haven where I really could bathe in chocolate if I wanted to, in my castle in the sky built on clouds of divinity. He presented me with the very first Xanadu Chocolate Decadence Bar as a birthday present.

He gave me the world, and I took it.

In a way, his exceptional generosity taught me how to take. And take, and take… until I was placing ridiculous demands on him just to see how high he would jump. Every time I took the bar up a notch, he cleared it.

Eventually, I was devoting my time to little else but trying to ruin what had become an essentially unbreakable relationship.

We are our own worst enemies: I became the worst of myself, and the dream girl that Xavier created betrayed him.

How were we together? I take it you're asking me what he was like. What do you think? Take the most grandiose, romantic version of what you've heard and multiply it times ten.

He was fantastic.

We were fantastic.

He understands children so well because he is one. He is a genius, but in so many ways he is still innocent. *Was* innocent.

He despises condescension, and he does not suffer fools. Life is too short. And magic was always drawn to him like a lodestone. His business cards should list Magic Magnet right beneath the Candy Man honorific.

There was so much magic permeating the air of that factory that nothing seemed out of the ordinary, no matter how strange. A tree that tasted like toothpaste. An edible flower that bloomed all the colors of the rainbow. I was approached by Minians who were: blue, gigantic, the size of insects, teleporting, invisible, flying. None of them gave me pause.

Much madness is divinest sense, after all.

Because of that, Xavier never ceased to be enraptured by the most mundane trivialities. Butterfly wings. Sunsets. The way rain slides down wet windows. Flickering candle flames. Wide, honest smiles and laughter.

Love.

Hope.

Honor.

Loyalty.

The Minians? Yes, he did always have the loyal Minians with their poetic souls, and he always will. You know that legend too, but again, my version differs slightly from the storybooks.

After the success of the Chocolate Decadence Bar, Xavier needed to expand his operations, and quickly. In his most humanitarian effort ever. and in some ways as a show of generosity for my benefit, he hired half the population of that small, backward island in the South Pacific to help him run his factory. Then, of course, the volcano erupted, the rest of the population (including all the women and children) were lost, and Xavier rose from Philanthropist to Savior in the space of a few horrifying hours.

Caught up in the romance and…gratitude, I suppose…I asked him to marry me.

I'm still not sure why I did it. I deserved him then as little as I do now. Three days later I took a job halfway around the world and had an affair, just to prove how little.

You asked me not to pull any punches, didn't you? If you want to think I'm despicable and evil, you go right ahead. You wouldn't be wrong.

But everyone falls short when measured against the Xanadu standard. He is too generous, too kind, too loud, too colorful, too smart, too funny, too wise, too understanding, to passionate, too…everything. He's a goddamned angel.

The rest of us, well, our heels hit the ground when we walk.

Maybe what I said before was true, and maybe one of those five other people on the planet is the perfect woman for him. And when they find each other, bells will ring across the globe and the world will sing about it and rejoice.

I won't leave the house that day. He does deserve his happiness. I just don't want to know about it.

Did I love him? Well, that's relative too, isn't it? I suppose, despite all the terrible things I did, that I loved Xavier as much as I was ever physically able to. I told him that I loved him; it wasn't entirely a lie. But it wasn't enough, of course. It was never enough.

Perhaps that's why I fascinated him, me without any hope or honor or loyalty, and completely incapable of the depth and breadth of love he needed.

Perhaps not.

How did it end?

I waited for him to do it, of course.

I wasn't completely stupid; I lived in a rainbow palace where every wish was granted, and every desire was edible. And I could have kept that world.

Instead, I just kept demanding more and more, taking and taking and holding the illusion of my love above his head until he finally, *finally* drew a line.

Condemn me if you will for how I ended it.

I think, perhaps, it would have been more heartless to stay.

Do I regret anything? Another hard question to answer. How

can a person regret being herself?

There are things I miss, of course. (I do not miss the Minians. I always thought they were creepy, the way they followed me around with their baleful eyes and haunting chants.) I miss the factory and it's nooks and crannies of adventure and instant gratification. I miss the way the world looked—as if all of us around him saw it through his eyes—full of light and color and soul. I miss the way the world smelled. The way it tasted. I miss the magic.

I miss…me. Or, rather, I miss the woman he thought I was. The woman he made me out to be. The woman I might even have been if the universe and my nature and everything else had been different. She was amazing, that woman. She was an incredible whirlwind of beauty and dynamite. She was talented and beautiful. She was full of hope and honor and loyalty and love, bottomless bounties of unconditional love. She believed in destiny, and life was her playground.

She was a dream, that woman.

I killed that dream.

I haven't seen him since that last visit halfway around the world—we kept up the pretense for a few weeks, but once the chocolate bunny fell, it was impossible to reassemble. He hasn't spoken to me since he found out about the affairs, and rightly so.

I still see him now and again—oh, not in person, of course. I see his face reflected on every angel in the architecture. I see his smile in every slice of lemon floating in a teacup like the teeth of the Cheshire Cat. I see his heart every time the sun paints the sky. I see the wonder of his eyes in every child who takes their first bite of a Xanadu Chocolate Decadence Bar. I hear his laugh when my daughter swings so high her tiny bare feet touch the sky.

I tell her that her mother was once a princess in a fairy tale. It's not entirely a lie. And when I hold her up so that she can catch the sun in her palm I tell her that she is one in a million.

I hope those odds never change.

A POOR MAN'S ROSES

At first, she sang to remember. It was a way to pass the long, dark time, a way to drown out the buzz in her head when the earth shook and the bunker rattled, a way to live outside the bars of her cage, to be a woman who smoked and drank, flirted and pined, flipped her pin curls and married a man for his car. Eventually, Patsy Cline became Kerri's reason for living. In five years, she hadn't found a better one.

"Good morning," said Stella. It was the only clue Kerri ever had to the time of day, or the notion that days passed at all. Stella opened the cage hatch and slid the food through. "I have a surprise for you today." She smiled. "You'll like it."

Let's see…what would she like? Kerri would have welcomed a hot poker in the eye, an asteroid hitting the earth, or the blast from that damned supervolcano the world had been holding its collective breath about for the past decade. It would be ironic, Kerri mused, if all three suddenly happened at once. About as ironic as someone surviving cancer just to live out the rest of her days in a prison.

"You're using your head-voice again," said Stella.

"Sorry." Kerri often forgot when she was speaking aloud, and when she wasn't. Stella seemed to be able to carry on the conversation regardless. "Surprise?" Beside her cardboard poultry and marbleized peas was a box. Kerri mentally dumped in that box all the bitterness she tried not to heap on Stella. The Bastard never had been able to make more than cereal and burnt toast, and his AI wasn't much better. Every time Kerri was tempted to advise Stella on how to make a palatable gravy, she asked herself why. Herself never had a decent answer.

Kerri lifted the box up to the laboratory light that slanted through the bars. "Animal crackers," she read...aloud? Stella smiled, so she guessed she must have. Then again, Stella was understanding more and more these days, whether Kerri spoke or not.

Surprise. Once upon a time the gesture would have meant something. Now, Kerri only felt empathy for the two-dimensional zoo creatures imprisoned by the lines drawn on their own cages.

"Aren't they wonderful? Dr. Petrakis brought them back on his last trip."

Kerri couldn't stop herself bursting into laughter; nor did she want to. Laughter told her she was still alive, and each guffaw brought her *this* much closer to insanity. *Oh, blessed insanity, why hast thou forsaken me?*

As if The Bastard actually gave her a second thought. "Doctor" Petrakis indeed. In this backwater life at the end of the world, you were whoever you pretended to be. There were no background checks anymore, and no point. No one begrudged another man his delusions of grandeur.

Fine. The Bastard could be a doctor; Kerri would be Patsy Cline. She put her fingers to her lips and took a long drag on an imaginary cigarette. "Wonderful," she said. "*Cra-zy,*" she crooned.

Perhaps insanity was closer than she'd thought. Thank God. Oops, no, wait, God left in the last exodus, too. For Mars. Or Europa. Kerri had forgotten which. Patsy was better company in the dark than God ever had been. All those Sunday vows broken on Monday. Every day was Monday now.

"They'll make a nice treat after today's session," said Stella. "Did you drink enough water this morning?" It was a rhetorical question. If Kerri didn't drink her minimum water requirement, the alarm would pierce her skull until she did. She ran her fingers down the needle tracks in her arm to the shunt in her wrist, connecting the dots into imaginary constellations, her map to a galaxy far, far away. That one could be a rose. Or a rabbit. Or a crashed airplane.

Kerri shrugged. "Sure."

"Fantastic!" Stella slid her knuckles across the doorplate so the scanner could register the microchip in her ring. Stella's response to anything was always followed with an imaginary "Whoopee!" Kerri couldn't fault the programmers; one could only laugh at comments like "The toilet is broken!" and "Guess we'll try another vein!" and "Looks like the world is ending now!"

Kerri felt the bolt pull back, a hum in her blood, before the door snapped open with a bone-scraping buzz of the same quality as her dehydration alarm, only briefer. Kerri counted down the thirteen steps to the purple chair. Sometimes she made it in seventeen. Sometimes she made it in nine. She was always walking, always after midnight.

"Let's strap you in," said Stella.

Whoopee!

It always surprised her how warn Stella's hands were. Kerri looked forward to the slight shock, the mass of long, dark hair bent over the tubes and dials that was so much like hers—dark like her daughter's might have been. Kerri closed her eyes and felt her essence flow out of those tubes like silken ribbons. It was Patsy Cline who kept her here, not Stella, not this android who might-have-sort-of-not-really resembled the daughter Kerri almost-maybe-never had. A daughter who played prison warden and stuck her like a pincushion and... She would *not* think about what perversions The Bastard did to Stella beyond that door at the top of those stairs.

That door at the top of the stairs squealed open. Kerri remembered the last time The Bastard had come to visit, so long ago; she still fell to pieces every time she saw him. Now, after all this time, he wanted to see how she liked her little gift. He wanted her to thank him.

Thirty-five thousand angels screamed in the hinges and cried in his shadow as he walked down, heavy step by heavy step. Kerri kept her eyes closed. She imagined seven chins, sausage fingers, a gluttonous stomach rolling over his waistband to hide his severely inadequate manhood. She saw the blackness inside him, the inkblots in his eyes that gave proof to the Elder God who had eaten his pirate soul. His cologne triggered her gag reflex. Stella squeezed her hand. Whoopee.

Ribbons, not blood. Red silk. A poor man's roses. A ball gown and a crown on her head; all ways about here belonged to her, and off with his head. Pins and needles. The straps bit into her thighs. She had lost enough weight for Stella to tighten them a notch.

"Hello, wife," said the voice that made her wish she had electrocuted herself a long time ago. Nanomeds be damned. Would that the cancer had taken her. "How's my golden blood today?"

Kerri opened her eyes and denied the angel she saw: wheat-blond hair, eyes as blue as the sky was, once. That flat stomach that did not have her spear thrust through it mocked her, teased her, tortured her. She wished she could take her own share of his worthless, mortal blood and watch it spread out on the floor, seep around the bolts and through the cracks, down into the worthless soil of this wretched world that the universe had balled up and tossed in the waste bin. The Bastard and this planet deserved each other. *Why are you here?* Her head-voice cried. *Why are you still alive? Why haven't you crossed the wrong person or been hit by a meteor? Why haven't you dropped dead from the evil inside you? Why hasn't the earth opened up and swallowed you piece by dark piece?* Stella looked sad. The bunker trembled as Kerri's heart cried gold coins into her husband's leather pockets. Aftershock. Or premonition. Or both. Nanomeds were magical things. They made the recipient slightly more than human…and any enterprising harvester slightly less so.

His eyes had cried for her once, one solitary tear, the first day he'd strapped her into that chair, the first time—she had thought— he'd sold his soul to the devil, and the first time he'd sold her superblood on the black market to those vampires. He had made her believe it was her idea, made her think that this selfless gesture was for him, for their future, made her believe he'd loved her even half as much as she'd loved him. He had played her from the beginning, even before he'd bent down on one knee and asked her the question she would always regret answering. He was all lies. He was a mosaic, made up of exotic, multicolored pieces of lies.

But that tear haunted her, that tear shed from those eyes that had looked at her in a moment of sadness. It was easier for her to live this unlife, to survive this pain, if she believed he was truly evil, that he had never had a soul, that he had never loved her. He wasn't a good enough actor to pull off actual emotion. What then, what was that damned tear?

"Have you ever been lonely? Have you ever been blue?" Kerri sang aloud, more for Stella than for herself this time. She wished her heart really *was* broken beyond repair and not fertile ground for more torture. Her mind continued its escape. Ribbons, not blood, poured out of her. Garters, not straps around her thighs. The toughest decision she'd make today would be which shoes to wear. Then again, not really. Red shoes went with everything.

And then the pain stopped. The blood stopped flowing. The straps fell away, along with her fantasies, and she was naked before him. "Surprise," he said. "Go, if you want to go. I wonder which of us will be the happier."

This time Kerri stopped herself from laughing. Always the head games with him. Always the gifts, absolving him of all wrongdoing. Even the way he had phrased the sentence—if she left, it wouldn't be his fault. Nothing was ever his fault. And now he gave her freedom? From underground cage to doomed planet. How magnanimous of him. Five years, blissful and blameless.

Kerri's head pounded. The glasses on the table shook as another contraction seized the planet sick with ague and ready to spew forth her boiling crimson insides. She could feel the nanos already replenishing the bits of her that she'd lost. She could feel the earth around her and the pressurized chaos it yearned to release. She could feel Stella beside her, feel Stella's love for The Bastard. But AIs couldn't love, so the love Kerri must have been feeling was her own. It made her want to vomit. She'd been so wrong, for so long.

The Bastard pulled the shunt from her. He collected the tubing, leaving Kerri to awkwardly bandage the hole in her numb arm with a stray scrap of rag. Not that she needed it; the nanos would heal that too, soon enough. "Stella and I are leaving," he said. "It's not safe here. Roger Garrison's offered us a place on his ship."

It had never been safe on this planet. The Bastard would only be leaving if he had gotten a better offer somewhere else, on someone else's dime. Kerri looked at the blood bag Stella held, not even half full.

"Oh, don't worry," he said, as if she would. "I've been injecting Stella with your blood all this time; the nanos have finally taken hold and started to replicate. I'll still have something to fall back on."

Worry? Why would she let herself worry? The feelings she shared with Stella suddenly made sense. Kerri braced herself on the IV pole and stood shakily before him. His height made her feel small. He didn't deserve a goodbye. He didn't deserve to hear her speak. He didn't deserve to watch her walk away. But he did deserve something.

Kerri slid the IV pole over to Stella—she didn't even have to use her head-voice. The nanos read Kerri's thoughts and transmitted them to the AI receptacle now pumping with her blood, her heart, her desires. With all the strength Kerri didn't have, Stella took the pole, broke it in half, and stabbed The Bastard in the heart.

Whoopee.

My blood, my daughter. You fool. He slid to the floor. She felt taller. *Now you know what heartache is.* She waited for the light in the blackness of his eyes to dim, just to be sure.

Kerri made her way up the stairs without a backward glance; Stella followed. Upstairs, she changed into some of Stella's clothes and packed a bag. She did not vomit in the drawers of Stella's extensive lingerie. She was proud of herself for that.

It was dark outside, and the air smelled like brimstone. She waited until they had walked at least half a mile before she sent her message to the wind. The nanos released the magnetic field she had been using to keep the bunker in one piece. With a rush the earth shivered again and imploded, crushing the bunker like a tin can, cleansing the evil that had been done there with elemental fire, and burying whatever love she'd once known in a coffin of black glass.

Now that she didn't have to hold that anymore, power flooded through her. The Bastard had never known her true potential, and before now Kerri had been too afraid to unleash it. He had only known the submissive wimp she'd been. He would never meet the woman she'd become. She was proud of that.

But while her blood could protect her, it could not save the world. Nor would it ever truly heal her. The pain would fade. Her strength would return. She would live, and she would not sail this next ship alone. That was enough. "Where is Roger Garrison's hold?" she asked Stella. "It's time to go." Time to move on, just like Patsy would have.

Stella took the duffel bag from her and pointed east. "This way. Not far," she said, her dark hair clouding around her alabaster face, making her look like an angel. There was a drop of blood on her cheek. His blood. Kerri wiped him away.

"Thank you, Mother."

Kerri picked at the rag on her arm and pulled off the makeshift bandage. She wanted nothing on her body that reminded her of him. She was in no danger of bleeding to death; the hole where the shunt had been had already begun to scab over. It was shaped like a tear. She tossed back her hair and started walking, following her angel across Hell. Walking, always walking, today, tomorrow, and forever.

RABBIT IN THE MOON

Once upon a time

I was a rabbit in the world of men

Flesh and blood

True and free

Camouflaged in light and dark

In snow and shadow

Overlooked and wary of danger

It was cold that winter's night when the woman appeared

Eyes white as stars, hair black as night

Blue toes, blue lips, blue lost and hopeless heart that mirrored my own

She asked the bear for help but he could not spare it

He needed his store to see him through the bitter season

She asked the fox for help but she could not spare it

She needed her milk to see her kits through their first steps

Though she did not ask for it I offered myself timidly

Offered my blood to slake her thirst

Offered my skin to warm her

Offered my flesh to give her sustenance

She smiled upon me with those stars through that night

And she was whole

She was a goddess, and I had saved her
She made me one with the moon so that all could share my generous heart
High above the world
White in the black sky
True and free
Camouflaged in light and dark
Forever safe, forever admired
Forever alone
But her love left me a tether back to the world of men
Should I ever need to return sometime
Someday

It was another winter's night when the rooster appeared
Dark in the light
A black shadow on the white snow
His head bowed, his wings humbled
His heart a mirror that reflected my brightness
Drawn to him I followed my tether
Back down to the world of men
I offered myself timidly though he did not ask for it
Offered my blood to warm him
Offered my heart to nourish him
Offered my moon's light to guide him
He slit my throat with his spurs and bathed in me
Until his feathers shimmered russet
He fed upon my generous heart
Crushed it to pieces inside a gizzard full of broken glass

He asked me to return to the moon

To set for him so that he might crow mightily with the voice I

inspired in him

I said yes.

And he was whole

I was a goddess, and I had saved him.

He left me there, one with the moon

High above the world

White in the black sky

Forever safe, forever admired

Forever alone

I learned too late there was no tether

No way to return to the world of men

And no need.

For I need only myself

True and free

Camouflaged in light and dark

In snow and shadow

In pride and shame

I am whole

I am full

And all may share my generous heart

THE WITCH OF BLACK MOUNTAIN

Letting Anthony Gentry get her pregnant was the stupidest thing Ennica Jamison had ever done. Hiking to the summit of Black Mountain to see a witch was the second. It had been a warm November afternoon when she'd left her stolen horse on the path at the base of the mountain; now it was cold and dusk. She placed a foot on the first step of the abandoned lookout tower. She'd been walking for hours, slow but determined, sprinkling what sanity she had left behind her like breadcrumbs in the dirt. She grasped the rusted orange railing firmly with a gloved hand. One last thing left to climb. One last moment before she discovered just how stupid she really was.

She stomped her boots hard on the metal to make sure there was no ice; each step brought one more inescapable thought along with it. Every time she closed her eyes, she saw herself stabbing Anthony in the heart—the heart he didn't have—so she tried not to close her eyes, but her mind still raced against her will. How he and that bitch Tanya must have laughed at her; how they must be laughing at her still. Her father would be mad that she'd taken the horse out overnight, but he'd be furious when he found out he was going to be a grandfather.

It didn't have to be a knife. Maybe a spear, like in the ancient days of Spartans and honor. Anthony wouldn't have survived long in that world. The dream of his blood pooled in her hands, all his life and all his lies drained away. No. Concentrate on something else. One more step.

She was high enough now to see where the elevation benchmark disc lay, the official plaque set in stone by the Geodetic survey crew back in the fifties. She had passed it fifty yards or so back and wondered if she'd been kin to anyone on that team. Probably. Over four thousand feet up…and two more steps.

Her panting breath froze her tongue, the fog before her reminding her of the surreally beautiful ice on the rock face a mile or so back. If she was ever crazy enough to come back this way, she'd have to bring a camera. If she survived. Three more steps. The tower creaked and shivered. It might have been her shivering.

It had been a girl in the schoolyard who had told Ennica about the lookout tower. "But built to look out for *what?*" she'd asked rhetorically, chewing on the end of one of her ribboned chestnut plaits. "I'll tell you what. My nanna says if you climb to the top of that tower, it'll show you where the witch lives." The Witch of Black Mountain, the dark fairy long ago cast out of the magic circle. The one who grants wishes and eats babies and who'll come and suck your soul if you don't put your toys away before supper.

Supper. Ennica couldn't remember if she had stopped for supper. It didn't matter. One final step, and she was at the top. She looked out over the clearing, scanned the treetops.

A lone crow drifted in and out of the mist on the early evening currents. Other than that, she saw nothing.

Ennica took a deep breath, sucking in more cold than oxygen, and blew out another cloud of fog. She wasn't surprised; deep down she'd known this was a one-way trip. Supplies would have just slowed her down. Her whole body was tired. She just didn't have the strength to walk anymore. They'd find her huddled at the base of the tower, peacefully frozen in her sleep. Or perhaps she'd just stay right here up at the top, the closest she'd ever be to the stars in this life. Spiritual, almost.

A sob escaped her; her chest felt like a mason jar about to explode. Her cry echoed over the quiescent landscape, unanswered by nightingale or Chuck Will's Widow or that ephemeral crow. Even the cicadas didn't dare infest this high. The night was a tomb. Fitting, really. She felt tears eke out and freeze on her lashes. She refused to be a wimp, especially if she was the only one around to witness it, so she blinked them away. *Blink.*

Anthony. Stabbed. Blood. Relief.

Ennica gasped and opened her eyes again. She wished she was brave enough to go through with something like that, brave enough to save the world from one more lying, cheating, thieving bastard. Hell, she couldn't even save herself. If she'd have lived through this, her kid would have been a bastard too. She didn't mind.

She put a hand on her still-flat belly. Hopefully it was warmer in there. Without closing her eyes, Ennica imagined she was sitting in front of a nice, warm fire. It smelled of cedar and coal and hand-me-down quilts. It blurred her vision and burned her eyes. She rubbed them, looking out over the mountaintop.

She wasn't dreaming.

Ennica followed the smoke trail back to its origin, and could just barely make out the silhouette of a rooftop among the trees. She memorized its location in relation to the tower before scrambling down, snatching her pack up, and hightailing it to the front door. She pulled off her gloves; her skin was so dry when she rapped on the door that her knuckles bled.

"Yes?" the soft female voice was followed by the furious flapping of wings and the cackle of a crow.

"I'm looking for the w—" Ennica stopped herself. "Witch" didn't quite seem the polite term. "—the dark fairy," she finished.

"Fairies. Bah," said the woman. "Blanton Forest is about four leagues west. If you want romance, you're on the wrong mountain."

"Romance got me into this," Ennica called through the door. "Now all I want's revenge." There was no reply. Ennica counted her heartbeats: One. Two. Three. Four. Five. When she got to a hundred she'd…she'd what, leave? She had nowhere to be. Here on this porch seemed as good a place to freeze to death as any.

She heard rattling, and then the door opened a crack. "Come in."

The cabin was small—only one room—with no furniture to speak of apart from a simple table and two chairs beside a squat black stove. Ennica fell to her knees before it, suddenly aware of how cold she was, and exactly how close to death she'd come already. The fire smelled of coal, wood smoke, apple pie, and lilacs. There. It was official; she'd lost her mind. But she'd suspected that the minute that low-down, dirty rotten liar had kissed her.

Lord bless the genius who one day invented the soap that could wash memories like that out of her mind.

"Sit," said the witch. She had taken one of the chairs at the table, the crow perched on her shoulder. Before the other chair sat a plain white teacup filled with water. Ennica pulled herself up into the chair and cradled the cup in her icy fingers.

"What's this?" she asked.

"Whatever you want it to be," said the witch. The crow agreed.

Ennica nodded and took a sip. What hit her tongue was not water but hot chocolate—not the weak, powdery stuff she'd drunk as a kid but honest-to-goodness cocoa, the thick, molten creaminess that rich people had for breakfast in all those books she liked to read. *See, baby?* she said to her womb. *This is what you deserve in life.* Not too bitter; not too sweet. It tasted elegant and beautiful, and as it coursed through her veins it calmed her nerves and warmed her bones, lulling her into a sense of comfort. She closed her eyes...

...and saw Anthony and Tanya, naked, passionately devouring one another. She mentally skewered them together with one thrust of her spear and shoved the vision aside. Damn them both. They were not going to ruin her chocolate.

Bravery reinforced, she opened her eyes. She'd doodled her fair share of witches on her notes in class; old and wizened and warty, sultry and buxom and irresistible. The woman stroking the silky coal-black feathers of the crow didn't look anything like them. She wasn't young or old. Her features and coloring were the averagest of average. She could have been any woman on the street. She could have been the clerk at the grocer's. For that matter, she could have been kin—she looked quite a bit like her cousin Jessica.

Ennica sipped her magical chocolate again. "I'm Ennica," she said finally.

The witch raised her eyebrows. "Interesting."

"I was named after my grandmother, Eunice," Ennica explained. "The nurse who filled out the birth certificate had terrible handwriting." Her words sounded stupid even as she was saying them. *Nice, Ennica. Now maybe we can chat about the weather and our favorite music and try on each other's clothes.* "Are you really a witch?" *Oh, well done there, idiot.*

The witch smiled.

"Sorry. I'm just…I mean, I meant…"

"Don't apologize," said the witch. "So few people ask the right question. For all your self-loathing, you're really quite perceptive."

Right. If she was so perceptive, she would have known that Anthony had never loved her.

"That's exactly what I'm talking about," said the witch, reading her mind. "Now cut it out and drink your chocolate."

She'd been raised to respect her elders…which she figured might as well include anybody who might have the power to turn water into chocolate. Ennica did as she was told.

"This is Mr. Hue," the witch introduced the crow, and it lowered its head to Ennica.

"Nice to meet you, Mr. Hue."

"To answer your question: No. We were here before witches were witches and words were words and the world was the world. Not Mr. Hue, of course, but the rest of us. We have been called the Wild Things, the Wrong Ones, the Widdershins, the Damps. We were the afterbirth; after Chaos came Order. We are the facilitators of that utter perfection."

"Chaos," Ennica repeated. "You're talking 'beginning of the universe' type stuff."

"A never-ending series of storms in a never-ending line of teacups. Life is Chaos. So it follows that we are Death." The witch pet the crow reverently. "He was once a majestic bird with rainbow plumage, Mr. Hue was. His first taste of carrion flesh turned him black. He is much more elegant now, don't you think?" She nuzzled his sharp beak with her nose. "Even more majestic."

The chocolate in her mouth turned to dirt, and Ennica forced herself to swallow. She had already welcomed insanity, or she would have never climbed this mountain in the first place. "Are you evil?"

"We are evil to good as night is to day and the end is to the beginning. We are solace and silence and solitude. We drew blueprints in the stars and fashioned this world from the dust, and we return all that thrives here to it. We complete the circle."

"By killing people."

"By bringing order to chaos."

"So…by killing people."

The witch shrugged. "As you wish."

"What do you get out of it? Power? Joy? Vengeance?"

"Balance," said the witch. "It is the way of things. Up, down. Life, death. Action, reaction. The reason we do what we do is because the universe could not exist without us."

"If you hate life so much, you must find me revolting."

"Not in such harsh words."

"Tell me then," said Ennica. "What do you see when you look at me?"

The witch studied her with strange eyes, bright in contrast to the dark shadows in the skin that surrounded them, but still flat, like the crow's, like the deer heads mounted in Ennica's father's garage. They burned like a fire with no flame. Like the coal, deep in the heart of the mountain beneath them.

Ennica imagined herself through those dead eyes. A short, pudgy girl with stringy hair and blotchy skin. A good heart and a soft life. A mouse in a field waiting for an eagle to prey on it, waiting to be wanted somehow, by someone. Desperate and sad and stupid and too full of dreams and fairy tales to be of much use to anyone.

"I see a mess waiting to be tidied up," said the witch. "I see a life within a life, and I pity you both."

If the witch could read her mind, then her knowledge of the pregnancy was no surprise. *Smile, baby. You've just met your first witch.* "If you find humans so unpalatable, why look like one?"

The witch folded her arms and crossed her legs under the table. Her feet were bare beneath her ragged skirts, but there wasn't a speck of dirt on them. "You came all this way to ask my story?"

"Look," said Ennica. "It's been a long day, I imagine it will be a longer night, and I have little left to lose. My mind's full of its own misery, and to be honest I'm tired of it. I would love nothing more than—okay, than my ex's head on a platter, but second to that, I'd love to hear about some troubles that aren't my own, you know?"

"I like you," said the witch with her dead eyes.

"I might like you too, but the jury's still out," said Ennica. "So spill. Why live the life of a human?"

"It is my curse," she said. The crow murmured a consoling caw.

Ennica picked up her teacup again. "Oh, this is going to be good."

"We were young," said the witch, "mere millennia old, a blink of an eye in the yawn of the universe. We were reckless, learning our boundaries, testing their resistance."

"Not so very different from humans," said Ennica.

"Only we lived deep down under the earth, in the soul of the world, in the heart of the mountain. Our paths were never meant to cross with the humans. And so it remained, until the humans discovered an aspect of our existence they couldn't live without."

"Coal."

"In our wake, we cannot help but arrange the basic elements into their purest form. Given enough time—"

"—the earth would be a diamond." Ennica's grandfather had been a miner. He'd taught her about coal, and its varying degrees of carbon purity. The purest carbon, given time and the pressure of the world above it, was a diamond.

"Unfortunately, humans evolved before that time had come to pass. They dug tunnels into our sanctuary and brought light and noise and chaos where there had once been silence."

In a twisted way, Ennica could relate. "It's never fun to have your once peaceful existence smashed to pieces by some uncaring lout."

"Exactly so. My siblings and I try and maintain our privacy when we can, in our way."

"Siblings?"

"The imp, the angel, the twins, and I."

"You lost me," said Ennica.

"You can always tell the imp's passage from his distinct odor. The angel has put so many birds to rest that she takes wing herself now, most days. The twins, they fight. Always fighting. They are the argument, and the cold shoulder."

"And you are the blackdamp," said Ennica. Her grandfather had told her stories of men killed by the damps in the mine. The stink damp reeked of sulfur. The whitedamp killed the canary before it killed you. The firedamp exploded. And the afterdamp got you when the dust settled, just when you thought you were safe. Then there was the mixture of everything, the queen of them all: the blackdamp.

The witch had called them the Wild Ones, the Widdershins, and *the Damps*. Ennica wondered what the miners would say if they knew it was vengeful fairies smothering their brothers to death in the bowels of the coal mine.

"I was always drawn to the humans; they were complicated beings, and so am I. They disgusted and repulsed me, but I was fascinated. I knew I should stay away, but I could not. "The witch cocked her head to one side, a gesture that would have looked more natural performed by Mr. Hue. "Does this make sense to you?"

Let's see: desperately wanting something you know you shouldn't, and then later being burned by same. Oh, yeah. She'd written that scene in her diary a time or two. "Yes," said Ennica.

"We are completely different," said the witch. "There is nothing of us in you, and never should be."

"Should?" asked Ennica.

"There is one thing." The witch raised a finger. "The spark. I would never have known it had I not seen it with my own eyes, for it was something I never would have guessed on my own. The Damps, we are one or we are many. We are legion or solitude, at will. We are here, there, and everywhere, or nowhere, as we wish." She looked pointedly at Ennica's stomach and Ennica raised a hand, as if to shield her unborn child from those dead eyes. "We do not procreate as you do. We simply exist."

"But you know about human procreation?"

"Yes. A man and woman once came into the mine, back when the tunnels were first being shored up. There have been many since, but this one…this one was my folly. They shed their clothes and came together and created a life."

Or ruined one, thought Ennica.

The witch's eyes glowed, and suddenly did not seem as flat and lifeless as they had before. Ennica wasn't sure it was a good thing.

"The spark," said Ennica.

"I witnessed it, that one perfect moment in the midst of all that chaos when two souls came together and merged perfectly into one. And it was…"

"…a miracle," said Ennica.

"But only for that moment," said the witch. "That one, blessed moment when your species and mine suddenly have the same goal: simplicity and beauty in one perfect unity. Not long after, that unity divided into two, and then four, and again and again, creating that thing"—she looked down at herself in her gray rags—"*this* thing you call a body." She touched her arms, the skin at her throat, her face. "How can you stand to be trapped in this prison, ever slowly succumbing to entropy?"

"How did you manage to become trapped in it?"

"I was caught up in the moment. Mesmerized. When the spark was created, my essence was trapped within it and I became its soul."

"You became that baby?"

"I became a spirit trapped in a messy carcass." She spat out the rancid words. "I did not become human."

Ennica did not want to upset the witch before she asked her request, so she kept her talking. "What happened to the soul of the baby that would have been?"

The witch blew across her fingertip as if blowing out a tiny candle flame. Though she was no longer cold, Ennica shivered.

"I was invincible. I was immortal. I was before time and after. I was perfect. And but for that one, beautiful, damning spark, I would be perfect still."

"So if you're no longer human and no longer a Damp, what are you now?"

Dead or not, Ennica recognized the look in those eyes: that same look she had seen in the bathroom mirror, splattered with the vomit that had ricocheted off the sink after she'd found out that…after she'd found out. It was a look of confusion, devastation, and loss. And as soon as Ennica saw it, it was gone. That blissful innocence had been replaced by something stronger. Something deadlier. Something…else. Something with the power to grant wishes, to tame crows, to climb mountains.

"I don't know," said the witch. "We were not meant to feel. We were not meant to love or hate. We were simply meant to be, until the end of the universe and beyond."

"You loved?" It was impertinent to ask, but Ennica could not help herself. In a way, she was jealous. She wished she didn't have to feel anything. How much easier her life would be right now if she couldn't experience the pain of love and hate, humiliation and responsibility.

Mr. Hue cawed again and preened himself. Had the crow been her lover? "No," said the witch. "Mr. Hue and I connect beyond trivial emotions. But I did love a man once, a human man. I yearned to hold him in my arms, to sink my hands into his flesh and watch him crumble to ash, to free him from the prison of life."

Ennica wasn't sure if she should be more worried that the witch spoke so casually of murdering her lover, or that Ennica herself wasn't moved by it. "You didn't kill him?" she asked.

"Worse," answered the witch. "I doomed him to live. I fled into these woods, as close as I could ever be again to the heart of my home, my mountain, and here I have remained."

"I'm sorry." Ennica reached her hand across the table to pat the witch's arm, give her some comfort in knowing that, for this little while at least, she was not alone. The witch's skin was cool and smooth, like marble. Like death.

Ennica bit back a sigh. Only she would be stupid enough to comfort Death.

"It is late for you," said the being to whom time meant next to nothing. "You should rest; regain your strength." She opened the door behind her, a door that had not been there until she reached for it.

The house was like the teacup of water then; it was whatever she wanted it to be. Nice. In the room was a bed, as simple a furnishing as the table at which they sat, but it would suffice.

Beggars can't be choosers. Still far and away better than slowly dying outside on the frozen ground.

The teacup was now gone, as was the table. And when Ennica stood to follow the witch into the room, the chair beneath her disappeared as well. Would that certain memories could vanish just as easily.

"I will grant your wish," the witch told her. Mr. Hue cawed his concurrence from her shoulder.

Ennica had never voiced her desire aloud, but she apparently hadn't needed to. "Thank you."

"For once, I believe it is I who should be thanking you," said the witch. "Sleep well."

Ennica did sleep well; her exhaustion caught up with her the moment her head hit the thin feather pillow. But her dreams were not sweet.

As before, the shadows on the backs of her eyelids resolved themselves into Anthony and Tanya. Ennica clenched her fists as she watched them conspiring, laughing, carefree without so much as a passing worry about the innocent life—lives!—they had ruined in their selfish wake.

She was not a fairy; she was no firedamp. She could not stand aside with a soul of vapor and a heart of coal and watch, indifferently, as she doomed her lover to live out his life. She walked up to the couple, her long black skirts swirling about her legs and brushing the tops of her bare feet. With one pale arm she pushed Tanya to the side, and with the other she swept Anthony up in her cold embrace and kissed him. Through that kiss she fed him all her love and all her pain and everything else she had in her that he never did—and never would—understand.

He tasted like chocolate.

She felt his heart stop, felt his body grow cold in her arms. She felt him crumble to dust beneath her lips until there was nothing in her hands but ash. She felt the rainbow colors of the baby inside her melt away into a majestic, elegant blackness. There was no noise, no mess, and the feel of the soft soot between her fingers was ecstasy. She knelt, thrust her hand in the pile of Anthony at her feet, and pulled out the one thing that would not have turned to ash: his spark. It was a diamond now, burning with a deep, pure fire, and Ennica marveled at its perfection.

The horse woke her, nuzzling her face and shoulder and nudging her into the sunshine. The house was gone; the witch was gone. She and the horse were alone at the base of the mountain. She squinted up at the sky, up the mountain path she'd have sworn she'd climbed the day before, and then she remembered how stupid she was, and how insane, and possibly how hormonal. She shrugged it off. A shame, really, that her little adventure had all been a dream.

She slowly picked her aching body up, moaning and cursing the unforgivable ground that had been her bed and wondering where the rocks had been that made her hurt so badly. She bent and stretched, trying to work enough kinks out to remount the horse; she should really get it back to the stables before her father started to worry. As for the rest of her life...she put a hand on her belly.

Odd; she felt none of her previous hatred toward Anthony anymore. She could honestly say she no longer loved him. In fact, she didn't feel anything. She closed her eyes...and thought of an abandoned watchtower, and teacups filled with chocolate, and a stove that smelled like apple pie. All those horrible memories and terrible feelings and atrocious, nonsense fantasies were gone.

"Thank you," Ennica whispered to no one, for if it had all been a dream, there was really no one to thank. As if in reply, a crow swooped down in a whirlwind of ebony feathers and dropped a shiny object in the dirt at her feet. Cawing triumphantly, it flew away, back up the mountain, into the mists from whence it came. Ennica bent down gingerly to retrieve the diamond, and the knowledge that came with it.

She would return the horse and say her goodbyes. She would not stay for the funeral or the gossip; that was some other girl's life now. That blissful innocence had been replaced by something stronger. Something deadlier. Something…else. Something with the power to grant wishes, to tame crows, to climb mountains.

She lifted her face back up to the path through the trees and the red-tinged dawn of the new day. Somewhere on that mountain, there was a cabin waiting for her.

THE GOD OF LAST MOMENTS

Max received the package from his mother three weeks after her funeral. She had come to him just the night before in his dreams; he'd scolded her for her continued attempts to meddle in his life. Without a word she had lifted great wings and flew away, a perfect image of the guardian angels she'd always sworn walked beside her. Such was the way of dreams.

The package, however, was not a dream. It didn't appear harmful or potentially hazardous. It was white and padded and metered with the correct postage. There were a few stamps and stickers and scuffmarks declaring its delicate nature and boasting of a long and possibly strenuous overseas journey, but nothing that gave any hint as to the contents or the intent of the sender. In fact, there was nothing particularly strange or unique about the package at all, apart from two slightly odd things.

The first odd thing was that the package had his name clearly printed on it above his mother's address, the address where he and Rose had spent the last few days clearing out clutter and deciding what to do with the rest of their lives. A decision Max would have been happy to put off for just this side of forever.

The second odd thing was that it was from his mother. The return address had been penned in a neat and steady hand, neither of which his mother had ever possessed. But there in blue ink was her name and a residence somewhere in Våmhus, Sweden.

Max didn't know where Våmhus was, exactly. For a moment he imagined his mother sipping coffee in a little café, fishing on a fjord, or lounging in a chair on the deck of a ship, laughing over how she had fooled everyone, wondering about the donated casseroles and the turnout at her graveside. But Max had been there at the hospital, had seen her corpse in that ridiculously expensive casket. He had watched the mechanism lower it into the ground and had thrown the requisite rose in after it. Max might not have been sure about what he had eaten for breakfast, or the weather tomorrow, or the contents of this mysterious package, but he was sure that his mother was most definitely deceased.

Still in semi-shock, he heard Rose's footsteps skipping down the stairs. It was always a hop and a skip and a gallop with her, never the steady, predictable rhythm of most normal people. Everything about Rose was ever-so-slightly off beat from most normal people.

In many ways, Rose was much like that mysterious package. On the outside, she didn't appear to be anything more or less than your sweet, average, chubby, middle class girl next door with long dark hair and rosy cheeks and a smudge on her chin. She might have just been making cookies, or enjoying a good tumble, or fixing the lawn mower, or all three at once.

Also like the package, there were two slightly odd things about Rose: the first being that almost unnoticeable social syncopation.

The second odd thing was the solitary butterfly clip she always wore in her hair. It was currently stuck in the side at random, slid to where the spirit moved it, and sparkling like mad despite the dust. That constant butterfly belied the presence of one foot still firmly set in a world of eternally optimistic girlhood. Rose, too, believed that angels watched over her from on high, that the universe spoke in fortune cookie riddles, and that there was always a bit of magic just around the corner. She even believed in him. Loved him. Max wasn't sure what supernatural force had prompted such unwavering, unconditional faith, but he wasn't stupid enough to turn down a pretty woman's heart, soul, and body when freely offered. There was also her obsessive love of strawberries. Okay, so maybe there were three odd things.

"Yay! I'm glad you got home before the storm. Did you pick up rags and polish? You did, you wonderful man." Rose often posed and answered such rhetorical questions. She had adopted this style of soliloquy so that the passengers on her train of thought would always know which station they were approaching, and which they had just left.

Max was not a wonderful man. But he didn't mind donning the clothes of the fairytale prince Rose decided he was, so he squeezed into those shoes every morning.

"I still feel uncomfortable opening your mail." She indicated the package as she moved to the sink to wash her hands. "Either you have a jealous girlfriend in Sweden you're not telling me about, or you're being stalked by a very sick individual. Or both." She smiled that enormous smile that had captured him all those months ago like a moth under glass, no doubt positing that the latter scenario would leave her much better stories to tell.

Rose nudged open the door of the refrigerator with one foot and pulled out a small bowl of sugared strawberries, her usual reward for a hard afternoon's work, a long-procrastinated task completed, or a particularly harrowing trip to the mailbox. Max could smell the red sweetness of her indulgence from where he stood on the other side of the table. "No, thank you," he said without looking up from the package, and then did when she cleared her throat. She was not offering her fruit; she was handing him his pocketknife.

"You always did like presents."

True; he liked presents as much as the next selfish man, but he hated surprises. A surprise implied that at a certain point in time, someone, somewhere, had knowledge of something he did not, and that feeling rankled him. A man should have control over his own life. There were traces of adhesive on the stout little blade. "You've been using my knife?"

"I needed it to open boxes. Don't worry; I'll clean and sharpen it when I'm done."

Max grunted. He sliced open the mysterious package and shook its contents out into his palm. It was small, whatever it was, and secured in enough bubble wrap to float the Titanic. Max set the blade to the translucent layers that blossomed beneath it. At the heart was a burgundy silk purse small enough to hold a large coin. But it was not a coin. Instead, the object was a coin-sized medallion, a tempered circle of glass edged and backed by what looked to be medium-quality silver hung on a length of dark twine. Etched in the silver was a crude, gowned stick figure with wings, some idiot child's rendering of an angel surrounded by four dots like an unfinished square. Something Rose might have scribbled in her younger days…or yesterday; the butterfly hairpin winked at him. He turned the medallion over.

There was a lock of dull brown hair trapped in the circle of glass; suddenly Max realized that the cord from which the medallion hung was not twine but finely-braided lengths of the same dun tresses. He knew that hair. It was his mother's. He was in the midst of recoiling from the grotesque ornament when the angel symbol touched his palm.

Time stopped, and Max received the real message his mother had sent him.

He felt a vibration, deep and basic as a heartbeat pulsing through him, emanating from the medallion. Some long-ago forgotten mysticism had preserved his mother's life force inside this piece of her, connecting them through their familial bond. Blackness enveloped him, warm, safe nothingness, and beyond it the faint beep of machinery. The beeping from his mother's sickbed. Max could almost taste the antiseptic in the hospital room around him. He felt knowledge, explanation, sink in through his skin.

Angels indeed. His mother hadn't just loved angels; she had been chasing them. If his dream had been any indication, she was trying to become one. Had she succeeded?

He knew the answer as soon as he asked it: no. She had stumbled upon her ability to sense this strange elemental power, but she had not known how to harness it or she would have shared that knowledge with him.

Somehow, through this amulet, she shared it with him now. In that moment, Max experienced his mother's frustration at coming so close to the secrets of the universe without ever achieving them. In that moment, Max knew he would succeed where his mother had failed. In that moment, Rose was yammering on about something. Max only stopped to notice when her curious fingers swam into his concentrated field of vision and plucked the medallion from his hand. There was a flash of brilliant white light and the warmth was instantly gone, the deep vibration silent in his bones. In his ears, Rose's voice resolved itself into words.

"Now I remember," she said. "Mourning trinkets. Hair jewelry. I read or watched something about this poor, small village in Sweden and the women who kept it thriving through their talents. On the History Channel, maybe. Queen Victoria was a big fan. Of the jewelry, not the History Channel, obviously." Her seemingly endless knowledge of trivial facts never ceased to amaze him, but now all he could focus on was that power, that precious, warm, golden power that she had taken from him. It had slipped through his fingers like the silk of the bag he had let fall unnoticed to the tabletop.

He held tightly to the memory, waiting impatiently for Rose to examine the fine detail, comment on the exquisite handiwork, and make another profound statement about Samson, lost art, and the determination of the female spirit. He was already forgetting the punch that had shocked him, the heat that had filled the core of him. When she paused to take a breath, Max snatched the necklace back. He pressed the angel to his palm, closed his eyes, and waited.

Nothing.

He might never experience that feeling again. He might have missed something in the lesson his mother had tried to teach him from beyond the grave, a lesson prematurely ended by Rose's annoying fascination with everything. Scowling, he felt Rose's comforting hand on his shoulder.

"You miss her."

A simple nod was far easier than confessing the overwhelming desire to return to darkness. In the pit of his stomach, in the back of his mind, he yearned to taste it again.

"It's beautiful. Your mother was beautiful."

Max had never thought of his mother as beautiful. Had she been? Was she now, vacu-sealed in her satin-lined coffin for a century-century's sake? Awaiting entropy or worms or whatever came first? Frozen forever in that silent grave to which she had so selfishly taken the knowledge he now craved?

He barely felt Rose's soft touch up and down his back, barely heard her words of comfort, recounted memories, the tale of the chest in the attic and how the mourning gift suddenly explained so much...

"Chest? What chest?" Max filled the question with false affection for his dearly departed mother. Rose gave a sparkling smile and a look that on any other woman would have meant mischief of a baser sort. But true to form, Rose took his hand and pulled him straight up the stairs and into the attic.

The precariously stacked piles of boxes and furniture had no rhyme or reason, unless Rose had simply moved objects around willy-nilly in her neverending quest for strange adventure. She deftly navigated through the leftovers from his mother's life to a low, cherry-stained box on the other side of the room. She knelt beside it and rubbed her excited palms up and down the thighs of her jeans. Max could almost smell the strawberry mixing with the dust there.

He shifted a Tiffany lamp and a weathered sock monkey and crouched on the balls of his feet beside her. "A what-type-of chest?"

"A hope chest," she said chipperly. "I always wanted one, but we couldn't afford it. A girl put inside her hope chest all the things she prepared for her wedding day." Rose lovingly stroked the lid, sliding her hands along the elegantly-polished wood, tracing the initials engraved there.

"Your mother must have loved this box; it's the most well-maintained piece up here." Rose's eyes rose to the ceiling, reading the engraving like Braille, seeing dreams played out on the shadowed wooden beams overhead. "Can't you imagine your mother as a young woman, kneeling beside this box just like we are, embroidering cushions and handkerchiefs with wishes and hopes for her future?"

Max could imagine no such thing. But Rose did, so he nodded. "That's the story outside this chest," Rose said more seriously. "Inside, however, are different stories. After marriage, I'm not exactly sure what it was she hoped for." Rose gingerly lifted the lid.

Inside the box was a horror movie.

Angels—those same stick-symbol angels—were drawn everywhere inside the lid: large, small, scribbled in ballpoint, carved with a penknife, painted in watercolors, fingerpaints, and possibly blood. Some were surrounded by the square of four dots; some were not. Some of the dots floated aimlessly, angelless, like invisible dice.

"What *is* this?" He asked as a way to gauge whether or not Rose knew anything about the angel sigil. She certainly hadn't felt anything when she'd held the medallion; Rose never hid her feelings. There would have been a discussion, a question, a cry, a laugh, or a scream. And she would have forgotten about her bloody strawberries.

Rose's response was to shrug a little, raise her eyebrows, and blow out a breath through pursed lips.

Good. That feeling, that moment, had been his and his alone. What was it inside him that made him long for it? Had a demon slept beneath his skin, dormant and still, waiting for this key to unlock its cage? Had this unnatural ability only just now passed to him from his mother, having left her now-empty vessel? Was he the next step in evolution? Max reached out to touch one of the angels on the lid. He closed his eyes as he covered one with his palm.

He felt nothing.

"Maybe the contents will mean something to you," said Rose. "Trigger a memory or something."

Or something, thought Max. *I want the something. I need the something.*

She handed him a clear, thick plastic zipper-bag. Inside were clothes—a woman's button-down plaid print top and khakis. Both were covered in either dried blood or rust-colored paint. Max knew which.

"Theresa," he said. "These belonged to my cousin."

"Is that...?" Rose asked about the blood. Max nodded. "Oh, wow."

Impatiently, Max slid the zipper open. "Car accident. Drunk driver. She was on her way home from work." He reached inside. "She was only—"

A shockwave hit him. The room swam away in a sea of blue, faded to red; a scream sang in his blood. He inhaled, tasted Theresa's fear, her surprise, the abrupt snap of bone, the adrenaline that washed over her, the wet, warm pulse as her blood left her, left her, left her body in quiet drumbeats. Then the world turned white. The attic room returned. Rose had placed her hand on top of his. Comforting. Waiting. Expecting nothing. She would have sat there for him, just like that, forever if he'd wanted her to.

Max swallowed the remnants of his cousin's last seconds on earth like a fine wine aged in a cask of blood, glass, and tires.

He blinked. He was staring at Rose, her dark-rimmed golden-brown eyes full of wonder and life. She was an empathetic soul, but she did not know what he had experienced in that moment or the overwhelming desire to feel it all again. More. She did not know; there was no way she could have known. It was his secret.

The thought pleased him.

He set the shirt aside and reached into the chest for something new. Rose folded the shirt delicately before returning it to the bag as if she'd always been so neat and didn't live out of a constant pile of her own garments tossed over the rail at the foot of the bed.

The roof settled with a crack and wind rattled the panes of the window as he debated which object to pick up next: a hatbox, a jewelry box, various papers, letters, pictures, a dried bridal bouquet. The oncoming storm roiled inside him; the charge of it raised the hairs on his arms, but there was no spark of electricity when he touched the photograph.

What filled him now was serene completeness and the deep, even breaths of a life well-lived. Eyelids heavy. Floating along the edge of the chasm of dreams in pursuit of the last dream, following it into the darkness, and knowing he was not alone. An ethereal presence comforted him. Urged him on. Then there was white again, and the sound of wings. *Wings...*

"He looks so much like you," said Rose.

Max focused on the picture pinched so tightly between his fingers that it was bent and trembling slightly. He went numb as the potent feeling seeped out of him, and he relaxed his grip. "This was my grandfather. My mother's father. Technically, I look like *him*." And his wife had died with this picture in her hand. Granna had fallen asleep on the couch and never woken up again.

He was on the verge of an answer. Pieces of the puzzle were falling into place, but he couldn't see the big picture and it frustrated him to no end.

"I'm sure it was very special to your mother," said Rose in sweet misunderstanding. She brushed her dark hair behind an ear before lifting a bundle of bright cloth out of the chest. Max would have admired her restraint had he not been absolutely sure she'd already done so the moment she'd opened the chest.

"Gorgeous." Rose unrolled the long mesh scarf. It was mostly peach, shaded to gold and crimson along its elegant length. She closed her eyes as she caressed it. "Do you know the story behind this one?"

"No," he lied. "But you should wear it. The rest can wait until later." Smiling with her whole body, Rose deftly wound the fabric twice around her neck. "It flatters you," he said, though it would have flattered more a thinner woman with fairer coloring and a less generous bosom. He closed the lid of the chest as solemnly as the casket of a sleeping corpse. He was sated enough now, stronger and more powerful than ever before. If he consumed the memories trapped in the remaining items he had no idea what might happen. Would he overdose? Would it advance his evolution? It would trigger Rose's curiosity either way. "I have some research to do before bed, and you've been up here all day. You need a break. You must be hungry. I'm starving." Oh, how he was. But not for food. He wasn't sure he'd ever be that kind of hungry again.

***

The storm hit just after Rose went to bed. Max shut down the desktop and surfed his laptop on the kitchen table until the storm knocked out the wireless. Rose was used to his freelance schedule: long days at cafés and research into the wee hours. Terrorists in Russian schools, earthquakes in India, tsunamis in the Pacific—as long as there was tragedy in the world, Max remained gainfully employed.

Now he researched his own dilemma. All the objects in question had been present at a time of death. Save the one from his mother, but that had physically been fashioned out of a piece of herself. *That* had been needed to trigger this supernatural power. Or had it? Had this power been with him his whole life? Max tried to think back on a time when it might have manifested itself. He must have encountered such objects before.

Or had he subconsciously kept himself apart from them? He

preferred new to antique. He never patronized auctions or yard sales. He abhorred gross displays of emotion and had subsequently avoided funeral parlors and nursing homes. He hadn't intended to visit his mother once she entered the hospital, but Rose thought it his duty. Unwittingly, he had gone his whole life without putting himself into the proper situations, and in doing so had completely hidden from himself what he truly was.

But what was he?

He spent hours reading page after page on death cults and cultures, natural selection and extinction, burial rites and stages of grief. There was a wealth of information on preparing for death and dealing with it, but not much about the moment itself. He found angels upon angels: harbingers of kindness, mischief, portent, guidance, justice. Spirits who gave dead men voices and led them to the underworld, gods who weighed hearts, and gods who guarded tombs. Gods who marked men for death, and gods who hanged them.

Max did not see himself as an angel. Perhaps he was one of those spirits, a mythical being. A death nibbler. A soul taster. A time collector. An as-yet-unnamed god of last moments. Only he did not judge or protect those moments, he consumed them. They thanked him and gave him their power.

He remembered the scarf. It stared at him from the other end of the table, lustily sprawled across a pile of books, unopened junk mail, and copious lists of things to do that Rose made and never consulted.

The second moment Max experienced had been more vivid since he knew what he was looking for, but that first one had punched through his virgin subconscious. It followed: the more violent the death, the more powerful the object's essence.

The scarf begged him to test that theory. If he was right, that six-foot scrap of stained sunshine would be the most important piece of the puzzle yet.

It was a famous family not-so-secret: Auntie Marie had strangled the life out of her philandering husband with this very scarf. That crime of passion, that madness-soaked murder, was worth being ostracized from her family and friends, locked away in a penitentiary for many, many years.

Max had a feeling…or rather, he didn't have the feeling just yet. But he wanted it. Oh, how he wanted it. It would be his and his alone.

Quietly he moved to the other end of the table. He took two deep breaths, rolled his shoulders back, cracked his neck. He planted his feet firmly on the hardwood floor, grabbed the scarf with both hands, and held on.

Sun boiled through his veins, searing him from fingertips to toes, burning away his vision of the dark house and branding it with some other place, some other time zone, some other time. It was molten joy and fear and sex and satisfaction, and he tilted his head back to gulp down the exquisite nectar. As this last moment played out on his soul, he was neither Marie nor her husband.

He was both.

The scarf: taut in his hands, tight around his neck. The blood: behind his eyes, in his ears. The bile in his throat, their throats. Two hearts beat in his chest: one speeding up, one slowing. Two screams: one in his mouth, one in his ears, both ringing with disbelief and betrayal, each from opposite sides of the looking glass. As one eye went dark the other turned bright. All the colors of the world merged into a pure, harsh, white blaze. And then he saw her. With that one eye he saw blood-black hair and dark eyes, striking against alabaster skin and her gossamer shift and the white white white of each feather that made up her exquisite wings and he wanted to be the ground she walked upon and the wind that caressed her and the tears that fell from her cheek and the fire that burned inside her being for all eternity and inthatperfectmomentgodhewanted—

Max awoke on the floor next to the chair, knees folded into his chest, scarf knotted between his fingers. The backs of his hands were tattooed with bloody crescents where he'd bit through the skin. He touched a trembling hand to his mouth. Blood there, too, fresh and wet and crimson. He was sweating, a cold sweat, and his mind felt…spent. Empty. Hungry. Starving again for that one answer he needed to find, the answer he now knew he was looking for.

Her.

He wanted her. She would fill him up and define him, give him life, give him purpose. She would love enough and live enough and burn so brightly that he would never be hungry again for all eternity. He was a hunter; she was his prey. He was a god. And he would have his angel.

He pulled himself to a sitting position, used the chair to help him stand. He patted his pockets on the way to the bathroom. He had everything he needed, but he should clean up first.

Ten minutes later, he put a hand on Rose's shoulder and shook her awake.

"What time is it?" Her eyelids fluttered. "Are you coming to bed?" When he said nothing, she sat up. "Max? Honey, is everything okay?"

"I need you to do something for me."

She shook off her dreams and suppressed a yawn. "Yes. Of course. Give me a second to come to." She put her hand, warm from sleep, over his. "My god, you're freezing. Really, are you okay?"

"I'm fine," he said. "I think I've just figured something out."

"Something about the hope chest?"

Interesting that it was the first thing she mentioned. The rest of the evening had not distracted her. That hopeless devotion of hers so often masked her intelligence. Thus remembered, Max would take care to tread extra lightly. "It's about Theresa," he said. "It's complicated—please don't ask me to explain. You'll think I'm an idiot. It will make more sense if I just show you."

"I love you. I would never think you're an idiot."

As it should be. Rose would never do a lot of things he did on a regular basis. "I need you to take me to the place where she had her accident. I can show you the way."

Rose leaned back, feather pillows crushing against the wrought-iron headboard, and sighed. "You *really* need to get a driver's license, city boy."

"I will, soon. I promise."

She dangled her feet off the side of the bed and took a deep breath. "All right. I'm up." She looked up at him with puppy-dog eyes. "Would you make me some coffee? Pretty please with strawberries on top?"

He gave her a well-deserved kiss on the forehead and was pleased to see her answering smile. She fed off his affection; he gave it out in small doses so that she did not gorge herself.

He made her a travel mug of "coffee"—it was more cream, sugar, vanilla flavoring, and kitchen sink than actual brew—and handed it over as she settled herself in the car. There was a chill in the night air; she'd put the scarf over her light denim jacket. She hadn't brushed her hair, but that damnable butterfly clip still nestled in her tresses. Rose pushed a button to the right of the steering wheel and the convertible's roof slid back.

"What are you doing?"

"Driver's prerogative," she said defiantly. "Storm's passed. It's a beautiful night." She put the car into gear and winked at him.

He gave her directions in as few words as possible and she was tired enough to respond in kind, mechanically turning to his instructions without question. When they were surrounded by scrub woods and well away from the lights of the city, he told her to stop. She eased the car to the side of the road and turned off the engine.

"So this is it?"

Max nodded. He had spent the entire ride, one hand in his pocket anxiously fiddling with his knife, thinking about what he was going to say when the time came. Perfect words eluded him. It needed to be more than appropriate. It needed to be poignant. It needed to be memorable. It needed to be right. It needed to be true.

After a prolonged silence, Rose's hand pressed against his cheek and he turned into it. Her tired eyes seemed wiser than the world.

"I love you," she said, which was better than anything he'd been able to come up with. In one fluid move he brought his arm up and sliced her throat. It was a swift, clean cut. She had sharpened the blade just that afternoon.

Rose opened and closed her mouth, unable to speak. Max tightened the scarf around her neck, absorbing the spray. Rose grabbed his forearms with both her hands and pulled at him, pushed at him, her voice a soliloquy of silent cries.

He knew what words she would have spoken. She would have wanted it this way. She would have been happy to sacrifice herself for his evolution, her final gift to him, a gift literally from and of her heart. She had been a creature of unconditional love, but something as trivial as love could never amount to his godhood. So she would be his means to an end.

Max did not grieve for a future that would never be. Perhaps he had loved Rose, as much as he could have loved anything. He was willing to accept that every event that had led them to this place had been brought about by the hand of fate, or destiny, or one of those mystical convergences Rose believed in but he had not. Until now.

As Rose's grip weakened, he looked into her eyes and saw himself mirrored there, saw her idea of him through them as well. He was at once the God He Was and the Prince He Never Would Be. But Rose did not see herself in him, in either direction. One could not see a place one had never been.

Love and strawberries; she bled out love and strawberries. Max was overwhelmed with the taste of her. His body spasmed with joyous anticipation. Her essence seeped from her body into his eyes and ears and mouth, filling the empty parts of him with her vintage, this time aged in a cask of his own making. Through her he drank of himself: his control, his benevolence, his importance. The memory held in the scarf was nothing; *this* was the most intoxicating spirit he had ever imbibed. It was the essence of a god. *This* was what he was meant for. *This* was the proper use of his power. *This* was what he had craved. He was not a spectator; he was a participant. He was the cause. He was a hunter. He was death. He was the creator and the controller. It was the first thing in his complicated life that had ever felt right.

And then he felt pain.

A fire burst in his chest, a heating blowtorch on bare skin that severed his precious link with Rose and stopped the feeding.

"Enough."

A tall, thin woman with a halo of fire-engine-red hair around a pixie face scrutinized him with flames in her eyes. Her voice was a crackle, a spark, a roar, brooking no opposition. The red woman leaned over Rose into the car, one long-fingered hand planted flat upon his chest. She burned him with that hand, burned him through his shirt and skin, burned him clean out of his body entirely.

Max's demon spirit stepped back, hovering over the gruesome scene in the car, insubstantial, a spectator once more.

The red woman wiped his flesh off her flaming hand onto her tight golden pants with a sneer of disgust. On either side of her, three men appeared from nothing, each taller than the woman, as if that were possible. One was lean, with hair like sky, eyes like rain, and skin like beach sand. His robes floated about him in slow motion, as if the air was more viscous where he stood. The fabric phased and shifted in a rainbow kaleidoscope. The second man was dressed as a simple woodsman, thick arms crossed over his barrel chest. His skin was the dry reddish-purple of a fountain pen Max had once owned, his arms and face marbled whorls of dark knots and wood grain, yet his hair was rosy and fair. The third man: bald head, bare chest, black goatee, one golden earring short of a bottleless djinn with murder in his stormy eyes.

These were the four then, the four dots surrounding the angels. The four elements escorting her. Which meant she would not be far behind. Max's spirit teeth gnashed and his tongue drooled. The fabric of the universe shifted.

His angel emerged from nothing and everything and shone like a star, blinding him with knowledge and illumination. She was a vision of extremes, both made of light and shadowed by its complete absence. Her wings were the down of a peaceful dove and the pinions of a raptor. Her soft brown eyes were a doe's and a wolf's. Her black hair burned with mahogany fire. He ached to have her, taste her, break her, bend her to his control, mold her to his desires, capture her and keep her and use her and sun himself in her divine candle all the way to immortality. But her guards would never let him.

He screamed his demon spirit rage to the skies, but though his teeth were sharp, his voice was impotent.

The woodsman reached down into the car with hard, heartwood arms smelling of loam and petrichor. He lifted Rose out, lifted her translucent essence right out of her blood-soaked and betrayed body. Her spirit clung to the man, face curled in his giant shoulder, arms around his neck, eyes staring fixedly ahead.

Max was glad those eyes could not see this new thing he had become. And yet—barring the considerable lack of substance— was it so very different from how he had been before? As long as there was tragedy in the world, he'd keep his belly full.

The man of many colors held his hand over Rose's hair, and the long, dark mass glowed with deep red, the same as the angel who now closed Rose's eyes for her. In turn, the other guardians each laid a hand on Rose's hair in a gesture of honor and empathy. The woodsman, whose hands were full, placed a kiss upon her brow.

As one they turned back to look at Max—not Max the cheap murderer sitting red-handed and limp in the passenger's seat, but Max the god-thing, Max the soul nibbler, Max the powerful, who by his own hand had extinguished a light that would shine no more. He stared back at the angel, searching her eyes for love. Devotion. Hatred. Fear. But she had no need of him. In her gaze was only the silent knowledge of who and what he really was. She pulled back the veil and he could no longer hide behind white lies and half truths.

He was but an imposter, a pilot fish, a beggar searching for scraps in the gutters of the road to the afterlife. He was a demon, a parasite, a poison. He had been a fool to think himself a god.

The djinn vanished and became wind. The true goddess spread her wings, and Max fell to knees he no longer possessed. The universe shifted again, and she was gone.

The guardians were gone. Rose was gone. The angelight was gone too, and Max was left with only the world in its plain, drab colors, a photograph flat and empty of the life her mere presence had infused.

Max hovered again above the bodies in the car. He wished he'd been able to at least hide the knife before he'd been so rudely excused from his corporeal existence. There it lay on the floor of the car for all the world to see, covered in her blood and his fingerprints, and Max helpless to move it. Whoever came upon this scene would have no doubt as to what had happened. If they only knew how these mystical events had transpired, how Rose's life had been willingly sacrificed in the culmination of knowledge gained after at least two lifetimes of research. But lo, no one would see that. They would only see the gory picture in blood-painted flesh before them, and their simple minds would jump to the simplest conclusion.

Max was rather glad he was no longer part of the idiot human race.

He turned to leave and something caught his eye: the butterfly hairpin winking wickedly at him in the dim starlight. It taunted with thoughts of fortune cookie riddles and magic and angels on high. It reminded him that there would be no more deaths by his hand. It promised him that Rose was so far away that he would never find her, even if he tried. This gift, his demon gift, would ever be his curse. He was now doomed to spend eternity hunting mortals on death's door and feeding off what he could steal. He would never know love. He would never be content. He would never be satisfied. He would never again taste strawberries.

Damn the butterfly. He would consume what moments he could and be powerful. He would meet his angel again.

His stomach growled.

He was hungry.

GHOST DANCER

She danced in front of the TV like an accusation, spinning and swaying and butt-wiggling in the space between his monitor and the television. She made a better door than a window. The bottoms of her white socks were gray with the dust and dog hair hidden in the ersatz wood grain of the laminate floor. She wrote a secret code into the steps, much in the way of bees, scolding him for squandering her brief visit and reminding her, even a little bit, of another man who had squandered her soul from behind a similar flat screen.

He let the half-hearted reprimand float away on the cool breeze past him and out the open window through which the Goddess growled at unsuspecting, lesser versions of herself. He pretended to ignore her, feeding the antagonism that would keep her at it, enjoying her enjoying herself. She had slipped effortlessly into the nooks and crannies of his life, scattered pieces of herself everywhere like rose petals in her wake. She was hammered into the silver nails of the dresser. She was shelved in between the eclectic titles haphazardly organized on the bookcase. She was folded into the clothes and tied up in the blind strings that pooled on the floor. She bloomed in the flowers he passed on his way to work, always happy to sacrifice a Technicolor blossom to sit behind her ear or wilt at the end of her braid. He could smell his shampoo on her long hair, strands of which he still found on his pillow. Her garnet earring was still somewhere in his bathroom, always there. He didn't try to find it.

They had shared blood and sweat and those brief days but no tears, a binding spell left unfinished. Instead there was talking and laughing and sighing and pouting and giggling and screaming and jokes about chaining her to heavy kitchen appliances that were only sort-of jokes about a creature of light and air who could not be tied down. And suddenly, there she wasn't.

He saw her still: a shadow just moved behind the bookcase, a dampness to his unused bath towel, a rumple in the bed sheets, a warmth at his back when the Goddess lay curled at his feet. It wasn't her face he saw through the bedroom window when he looked back up over his shoulder in the foggy morning. It was mayflies gathering at the screen and not tiny bubbles being blown through it, but he could imagine them, a parade of ephemeral fairies that would have made her smile and wrinkled the freckles on her nose. She still danced between his monitor and the television, twirling with the dust motes in eddies of air made by the cool breeze. She made a better window than a door these days.

THE MONSTER & MRS. BLAKE

Jeremy Blake took a snorkel to bed. An eleven-year-old boy was way too old for such nonsense, but he didn't know what else to do. There was a monster under there. A big one. And it was going to kill him.

He hadn't given the monster a name, like Jabberwocky or Wendigo or even Boogeyman. Mom always said that naming your fear made it real. Like having a pet. Once it had a name it was part of the family, for better or worse.

The monster had been with Jeremy since he was little. It started out as a shadow, haunting the corners of his eyes and scaring him into bed every night. It had stayed in that form for years before the noises came—a scratching at the window, the creaking of the closet door, deep, soft breathing. Like a cat's purr. A big, evil cat.

By the time Jeremy was nine, the monster was strong enough to move the bed. It liked feeding off his fear in the wee hours of the morning. Then it started to feed off his flesh. If he left his foot outside the covers, the monster bit at his toes with its many little mouths and tiny pointed teeth. If he rolled over and left his side exposed, the monster would scratch him from hip to armpit with its razor-sharp claws.

It hadn't left a mark…yet. But some days, Jeremy's feet were a mass of pins and needles that forced him to limp to the bus stop. Some days, his side hurt so badly he couldn't raise his hand in class to answer questions.

He could only hide under the covers for so long. It was only a matter of time before the monster became smart enough to catch him, strong enough to lift the covers, and real enough to kill him.

He couldn't tell anybody – who'd believe him? They would say that monsters don't exist, like Santa Claus and the Easter Bunny. Yeah. Only Santa didn't want to skin you alive and lick the blood off your bones, and the Easter Bunny didn't want to snap you in half and suck out your insides like a crawfish.

Baggy-eyed and sleep-deprived, Jeremy suffered in silence. He straightened the shiny, stiff baseball glove at the top of his bed. His eleventh birthday was two weeks ago. He wished he'd enjoyed it more; he knew he'd never see his twelfth.

Most days, Jeremy pretended he was a normal kid. He went to school. He played baseball with his friends. He helped Mom clean up after dinner, when Dad retired to the living room to watch TV.

"Jeremy, can I talk to you for a sec?" Uh-oh. It was the Mom Voice. She took the half-empty bowl of fruit salad from him. "Have a seat."

Jeremy shot a glance in the direction of the living room. When he heard the *Jeopardy* theme, he relaxed a little. A one-parent conference then. Whatever trouble he was in couldn't be that bad.

Mom smiled as if she could read his thoughts, and then scowled again. She picked up a fork and stabbed at an orange wedge, mad at the orange rather than mad at him. Mom was a bit of a nutcase, but for the most part, she was all right.

"Your midterm report card came in the mail today."

Jeremy winced.

"See, I have this problem," she said. "I'm a mom. Moms worry about their kids." She put the fork down. "I'm worried about you, kiddo. This isn't like you."

Jeremy shrugged. "I'm okay, Mom."

"You're not okay," she said. "And I have Mom Eyes, so you look ten times worse to me." Jeremy laughed. "You started middle school this year. Is it that? Is it the pressure of being the small fish in the pond again?"

"No," said Jeremy.

"I know some teachers don't like smart kids. I had my share of those when I was your age. If some teacher's taking it out on you, let me know. I'll beat the snot out of her."

The thought of his tiny little mom taking on anyone was funny. And not a little bit scary. "No, my teachers are fine."

She rested her chin in her hands and batted her eyelashes. "Is it a giiiirl?"

"Ma!" Jeremy started stacking plates.

Mom sat back in her chair. "Is it the monster?"

Jeremy knocked over his milk glass. What little was left soaked into the tablecloth before he could throw a napkin over it. He had told his mom about the monster once, years ago. He hadn't expected her to remember long after he should have grown out of it.

"It's all right, kiddo."

The hand she put over his was soft and steady. Jeremy flinched, ashamed of his own trembling. "I can handle it. I'm handling it. Just"—he looked toward the living room again—"don't tell Dad, okay?"

She chuckled. "Your dad's a bit of a monster himself, isn't he?"

"Mom, I'm not joking."

"Okaaaaay…" she started. Jeremy could hear the "but" coming like a freight train a mile away. "…but only if you promise to listen very carefully to what I'm about to tell you."

Jeremy reluctantly plopped back down in the chair.

"Are you listening?"

Jeremy nodded.

"Sometimes in life there come things that are just plain-old too big for one person to deal with." Mom pushed a strand of curly dark hair out of her pixie-like face. Jeremy would miss her when he was gone. "There's a reason there are six billion people on this planet. We're supposed to help each other out. There will still be lots of things you're meant to do on your own. It's part of growing up. But sometimes…" She sighed. "I want to help you, Jeremy. But I won't. Not unless you ask me first. Just promise me you'll ask me."

"I promise," Jeremy whispered. He would *not* cry. He would *not*. He might not have been big enough to scare away the monster, but he was big enough to resist *that*.

She kissed him on the forehead and tousled his hair. "Don't worry about the mess tonight. I'll take care of it." She put her silverware on top of his stack of plates. "Go on upstairs and try to get some rest. You look like crap."

Jeremy smirked. "Gee, thanks, Mom."

"Hey." Jeremy turned just in time to catch the apple she threw at him from the centerpiece on the table. "Midnight snack," she winked. "Love you, kiddo."

God, she was so weird. "Love you too, Mom."

What on Earth was he going to do with an apple? He wasn't supposed to eat in his room. If he got hungry in the middle of the night, he'd just go down to the kitchen…assuming he could let his feet touch the floor…

Huh.

Jeremy polished the apple against his shirt. Maybe his mom wasn't totally Looney Tunes after all.

He put the apple on his headboard next to his shiny new baseball glove. He got his pajamas and the snorkel and cocooned himself under the blankets. He said his prayers just like he did every night, with special emphasis on the "If I should die before I wake" part. It was rare, but some nights, the monster left him alone. He prayed this would be one of those nights.

It wasn't.

Jeremy woke to grumbling and gnashing teeth, the slurp of spit and the crunch of bones. He pulled himself into a ball and checked all of his limbs. In the blessed relief after his physical inventory, Jeremy realized that the crunching wasn't bones at all. It was the apple.

He smiled so hard he thought his face might break. If the monster liked fruit more than it liked him, it could have all it wanted.

Jeremy started taking an apple to bed every night. Mom never said a word. Red, green, yellow— she bought apples by the bushel and kept every bowl in the kitchen stocked. Jeremy got sleep. He did his homework. He passed his tests. He broke in his new baseball glove. He ate his meals with gusto and cleaned his plate in ten seconds flat.

"Drink your milk, son," Dad said, "so you can grow up to be big and strong like me."

Grow.

The monster had nibbled at Jeremy before, but it had never actually eaten anything. What if it was *growing*? What if, by feeding it, Jeremy was making the monster stronger than ever? What would happen when apples didn't fill it up anymore, and it wanted Jeremy for dessert?

That night, the monster bit Jeremy on the toe. Through the sheet. In the morning, there was a hole. The next night, a tentacle brushed across the bottom of Jeremy's foot. It left a welt. The claws left red stripes down his chest and across his legs. The little mouths left bruises and small puncture wounds.

It hurt to put on clothes. Jeremy took to wearing a hat and long sleeves, even when it wasn't cold outside. Each step was slow and painful and reminded him of what a coward he was. What a silly little boy. Eleven years old and still scared of the monster under his bed. What a baby. He knew that's what they'd say. If he'd been in their places, that's what he would have said.

True to her word, Mom said nothing. She and Jeremy cleaned the kitchen after Dad left, just like always. Sometimes she tried to make him laugh. Sometimes they worked in silence. But every night, when they were done, she handed him an apple and sent him off to bed.

"Mom," Jeremy said finally. "I'm asking."

She dropped the apple she held and took Jeremy into her arms. "Thank *God*! I was afraid you were going to wait until your school called and told me to stop beating you."

"You still won't tell Dad, right?"

She locked her lips and threw away the key. "Mum's the word. Go on, now. I'll be in after I put your father to bed. Don't worry, kiddo," she said. "We'll beat this thing."

Jeremy wasn't so sure. For one, Mom was *small*. He was as tall as she was, and he was only eleven! For two, she didn't know how huge the monster was. Or how strong. Oh, *no*. Jeremy didn't know Mom's plan for the monster, but he wasn't going to let it hurt her.

He did as he was told and went to bed. He picked up a book and turned the pages, too distracted to actually read. Mom showed two hours later, dressed all in black, with a green bookbag. "Jeremy, are you still up?" she scolded overdramatically. "You put out that light and go to sleep, young man." She waved her free hand in the air at him.

What? Oh! She wanted him to play along. "Aw, Ma…five more minutes?"

She gave him a thumbs-up. "No, sir! Lights out."

"O-kay."

Mom kissed Jeremy loudly on the forehead and laid the bookbag on the bed, close to his body. "G'night, kiddo."

"G'night, Mom."

She closed the door, tiptoed back to the bed, and eased on to it gently until she sat cross-legged, facing Jeremy. Moonlight fell into a square on the covers between them. Mom quietly emptied the bookbag into the square. There was an apple, a big knife, and a tape recorder.

Jeremy was confused. Mom put a finger to her lips. *Relax*, she mouthed. Jeremy fluffed his pillow and rested against the headboard.

After about ten minutes of complete silence, she pressed "Play" on the tape recorder. Slow, even breathing filled the room—the sound of someone sleeping. The sound of *him* sleeping! Jeremy sat up. Was that really what he sounded like? When had Mom taped him sleeping?

He opened his mouth but she scowled, so Jeremy listened to himself sleep. It was kind of funny. Every so often he murmured or rustled the bedclothes. He was so caught up in listening, he almost didn't see the hand reaching for the apple.

Jeremy slapped his hands over his mouth and swallowed a scream; tears sprang to his eyes with the effort. He'd never seen the monster when he was wide awake. Its fingers were large, with purple and yellow stripes. Blue-green veins pulsed under pimply skin. At the tip of each finger was a small mouth, each with hundreds of tiny, glistening, pointy teeth.

Having Mom there should have made it easier. It didn't. It made him more afraid—the most afraid he'd ever been in his whole life. The monster was real. Jeremy was going to die. And when it finished with him, it would kill his mother.

The arm slithered to the center of the bed where the apple lay. Two tentacles joined it. Jeremy refused to wet the bed and embarrass himself in front of his mother. Mom. At least he could see her wonderful, lovely, crazy face one last time before he died, could see her…wink at him.

Like lightning she grabbed the monster's arm with both hands. "Gotcha!"

"What are you doing?" Jeremy screamed.

The arm wriggled madly. The tentacles disappeared back under the bed. "Jeremy, help me!"

He didn't give himself time to think about how nuts this was. He threw himself on top of the monster's slimy arm and hugged it to him.

"Come out from under that bed!" No one disobeyed the Mom Voice.

The arm thrashed and writhed. Jeremy expected the monster to come out and attack them both head on, but it didn't. It kept trying to hide back under the bed. What did *it* have to be afraid of? Didn't it know it was bigger than Jeremy and his mom put together?

Awestruck, Jeremy watched Mom brandish the knife and cut off one of the monster's fingers. It growled and howled. The bed shook mightily. Green blood oozed onto the bedsheet and the smell of rotten eggs filled the air.

"Come out right now," said the Mom Voice, "or you'll lose another one."

The arm stopped moving. The howling changed into a whimper. Slowly, the monster eased itself out from under the bed.

Jeremy watched through squinted eyes. Half of him didn't want to see. Half of him couldn't look away. The reality of the beast was worse than he ever could have imagined. It had two hands with ten—now nine—mouthfingers full of teeth. It had two hands with four claws apiece, each one as big as Jeremy's head. The claws on its feet were even bigger. It had two eyes on stalks and four tentacles, two on either side of its body. And in the middle of its torso, like an octopus, was an even bigger mouth—one Jeremy could imagine fastening onto his head and sucking his skull dry. Or swallowing his mother whole. The monster's eyestalks swiveled to Jeremy. Saliva dripped from the big mouth.

"Jeremy, stop it!"

Jeremy tore his eyes from the monster and concentrated on his tiny, crazy mom with the big, shiny knife. Green blood slipped off the blade and onto the carpet.

"Now," Mom addressed the monster. "Do I have your undivided attention?"

The monster nodded. At least, Jeremy thought it nodded.

"You're hurting my son. It's one thing to scare him, but it's another thing to attack him physically."

The monster whined.

"I know you're just doing your job, but this has gone too far. You have to understand, Jeremy has a *very* big imagination. He gets it from his mother."

For some reason, Jeremy suddenly felt very proud of himself.

"I am not going to force him to be anything less than he is just to rid the world of something like you. However, I cannot allow this to continue. You are simply too frightening for Jeremy to imagine you into existence. As I see it, you have two choices. Go away forever," she lifted the knife again, "or we kill you right now."

The monster bowed. It closed its eyes. Ever so slowly it began to shrink. The edges of it blurred and folded in on itself. It grew smaller and smaller until it was only a shadow and a growl, until it was nothing more than a memory and a rustle of leaves outside the window.

Mom's shoulders sagged and she dropped the knife onto the bedspread. Jeremy threw himself into her arms, hugging her tighter than he could ever remember hugging her before. He couldn't cry…but he couldn't seem to speak, either.

Mom squeezed him back. "It's okay, kiddo. We beat it. Together."

Jeremy couldn't stop trembling. He was going to have a twelfth birthday. He could ask for a bat to go with his glove. It was going to be so much more than just "okay."

"You think you'll be able to sleep now?" Mom asked. Jeremy sniffled and nodded again. "Just toss that top sheet on the floor and I'll throw it in the wash tomorrow. And crack your window a little…it stinks in here." She collected the knife, the apple and the tape recorder and put them all back in her bag. She helped Jeremy into bed, tucked the bedsheet around him, and smoothed his hair back, just like when he was a baby. He let her.

Jeremy smiled up at her, his mom, the Coolest Mom in the Whole Wide World.

"Thanks, Mom."

"Anytime." She kissed him on the forehead. "Sweet dreams, kid——" She stopped herself. "Little man."

"Mom?" Jeremy stopped her before she closed the door. He had to know.

She poked her head through the crack. "Yeah?"

"The apples and the tape recorder and…well…how did you know how to do all that stuff?"

"Easy," she grinned. "How do you think I met your father?"

ALLIGATOR BABY

Marie slowly pushed open the door to the antique shop, gently disturbing the silvery bells that hung from the inside handle. The heavy Louisiana sunlight split the darkness, sparking the mites in the old air like fairy dust. Marie shut the door behind her and waited for her eyes to adjust. The room smelled of age and incense and magic.

She reminded herself to be brave. She was the bravest twelve year-old she knew, and she suspected that was so simply because she reminded herself so often. She had been brave enough to stay alone in the cotton fields all night long when she had gotten lost as a child. She had been brave enough to climb the tree on Devil's Island and win Big Andre's friendship. And she was brave enough now to walk right up to Voodoo Lily and ask the question that she had been wanting to ask her whole life.

"You gwan hide back there, bebe, or you gwan come chat?" a voice chuckled from the back of the room.

Marie forced one foot in front of the other and made her way into the shop. She was careful to keep her hands in front of her, her fingers clasped tightly around the handle of her small bucket. Oil lamps kept the room dim, and she didn't want to touch anything for fear the mountains of trash that surrounded her would avalanche and bury her alive.

The woman at the back of the shop was so large her hips spilled over the edges of her chair. Her skin was black as alligator mud beneath her red print house dress. Her soft breasts and belly jiggled when she laughed, bouncing the broken eyeglasses that rested there. Her eyes and teeth were white as cottonballs in the darkness. At her feet, a chicken with red and gold feathers pecked at the latch-hook rug.

"You gotsa name, bebe?" Voodoo Lily asked.

"Marie," said Marie, only the word had no voice behind it. She swallowed hard. "Marie," she said again, "Miss Lily, ma'am."

"Lees you gots manners," said Voodoo Lily. She tossed a handful of cracked corn on the rug beside the chicken. "Her name's Mustard," she told Marie. "She talks to angels."

Marie was too scared to do anything but nod. Andre said that Voodoo Lily had a way with animals…and a way of turning people into them. She wondered if people got to choose what animal they turned into. Marie looked down into her bucket. Probably not.

"That for me?" Voodoo Lily asked. She pointed to the bucket in Marie's hands.

"Yes ma'am," croaked Marie. She wasn't doing very well at this. She hoped she could at least make it long enough to ask her question before she turned tail and ran. The fact that Andre had promised her he would make fun of her for the rest of her life kept her frozen in place. Promises meant business.

"They're crawfish," said Marie, a little more smoothly this time.

Voodoo Lily smiled again, her teeth lighting up the room better than the lamps. "Jess fine," she said. "Thass jess fine."

Marie stepped forward quickly and set the bucket down beside

Voodoo Lily's chair. She jumped back just as quickly, startling the chicken with a squawk. Andre had told her to stay more than an arm's length away from Voodoo Lily at all times. "She'll snatch a hair from your head," Andre had said, "or snip a ribbon off your dress. And then she'll be able to do spells on you for the rest of your life."

"I have a question," Marie blurted out.

Voodoo Lily nodded solemnly. "Lemme look at you, bebe." She lifted the pair of broken eyeglasses off her breasts and balanced them on her wide, flat nose. She pursed her lips. "You wanna know 'bout mere and pere, eh, bebe?"

Marie's jaw dropped open. Voodoo Lily spread her legs and leaned forward, the chair creaking under her girth. "Mustard talks to angels," she whispered, "but them angels, they talks to me."

"My mama and papa," Marie whispered back, "are they angels?"

Voodoo Lily chuckled and the glasses dropped back down to her pillowy breasts. "They's dead folk, chil'," she said. "Them angels, they herd dead folk like shepherds herd sheep."

"Oh," Marie's face fell in disappointment. "I was hoping—"

"You was hopin' I could make some magic, eh, bebe?"

Marie nodded.

"Well," Voodoo Lily leaned back in her creaky chair. "Sometimes you gots to make the magic yoself."

"Myself?" Marie asked incredulously. "But I don't know the first thing about magic."

"E'erbody's got a bit of magic," said Voodoo Lily. "They's jess too busy most days to notice." She pointed to a table in the corner. "Fetch me them shoes, bebe. I show you what I'm talkin' 'bout."

Marie had to step over a white-gowned dolly in a rotting cradle and skirt a rusty washbin that looked to be full of old aprons, but she finally made her way to the table in question. It was covered in cigar boxes and cloudy mason jars full of spider webs. There were napkin holders and candlesticks and what looked like a small, brass monkey, but no shoes.

She stepped back and looked under the table. There were piles of old books, papers and magazines. On top of one of the piles was a pair of wooden shoes. She held them up. "These?" she asked.

"Yes ma'am," said Voodoo Lily. "You bring them shoes right over here."

Marie obliged, hugging the shoes to her as she navigated her way back through the labyrinth of junk.

"Now put them on," said Voodoo Lily.

Marie held the shoes out. "Put them on? But they're far too big for me," she said.

"You gwan tell Miss Lily how to do magic now?"

Marie snapped to attention at Voodoo Lily's tone. "No, ma'am," she said. She slipped off her sandals and slid her feet down into the toes of the hard, wooden shoes. There was so much room leftover in each one, Marie could have fit her fists inside behind her heels.

"Thass it," smiled Voodoo Lily.

"That's it?" asked Marie. "What's it?"

"You wear them shoes all day and all night," said Voodoo Lily. "Don't you never take them off. You bring them back to me tomorrow 'fore the rains come."

"And if I do this," asked Marie, "I'll somehow be able to see my mama and papa?"

"If you believe," said Voodoo Lily, "then them angels, maybe they talks to you too."

***

"She's nuts," Marie said to Andre. They sat under the pecan trees with the ice cream cones they had picked up at the corner store after Marie's visit to the antique shop. Andre paid with the money his Unca James gave him for working in the fields. It was too hot for ice cream, but that hadn't stopped them. They just licked at the drops that ran down the sides until they were down to the sugar. Marie ran her tongue over her fingers to catch one, tasting chocolate, sweat, dust, and the faint flavor of crawfish.

Andre ran his big tongue over his mint chocolate scoop and raised his dark, bushy eyebrows at her. "Then why you still wearing 'em?"

Marie shrugged. "Maybe she's not nuts. The only way I'll know for sure is to do it." She lowered her cone. "I want to see my parents, Andre."

Andre concentrated on his ice cream. "Mama Boudreau says you ain't got no parents," he said. "She says she found you out on the levee after the rain like a alligator baby."

"I ain't no alligator baby," Marie said defiantly.

Andre bit into his cone. "You seen anything yet?"

"No," said Marie half-heartedly.

"You heard any angels?" he smirked.

"You want this ice cream upside your head?" Marie asked sweetly.

Andre laughed. "Thass why I like you, little Marie," he said.

"You may be pint-sized, but you don't take nothin' from nobody."

Marie slurped her ice cream and took the compliment for what it was. "Thank you."

They finished off their cones in silence and wiped their fingers on the thick grass.

"You try walkin' through graveyards?" Andre asked finally. "Maybe them angels hang out there. You know, to shepherd the dead folk."

Marie stood up and brushed off her skirt. "I haven't yet. You think I should?"

Andre squinted up into the bright blue sky. "You sure it's gonna rain tomorrow?"

"Voodoo Lily said I have to bring the shoes back before the rain."

"Good," said Andre. "Means I get a day off from checkin' cotton." He put a lanky arm around Marie. "Come on. I'll go with you."

They spent the rest of the day walking. They visited graveyard after graveyard. They walked along the levee and back across the fields to Mama Boudreau's catfish pond. They had not seen one dead person or heard one angel. Marie was irritable with frustration, and from the clothes that stuck to her skin and the blisters that were beginning to form beneath her toes. But she wouldn't take the shoes off, not even when Andre dipped his own feet into the cool pond.

"I'll wear them to bed tonight," said Marie from the shade of the willow tree. "Maybe I'll dream about mama and papa."

Andre splashed his feet in the water, scaring the turtles that had poked their heads up in curiosity. "Maybe you'll dream about alligators."

Marie threw a rock at him, but only half-heartedly, and it landed with a "sploosh" beside him.

"Seriously though, Marie," Andre turned back to her. "I want you to promise me something."

"What?"

"If you wake up in the morning and you haven't heard nothin' or seen nothin'," he said, "I want you to bring them shoes back."

Marie plaited the grass at her feet. "I have to bring them back anyway," she said.

"And after you bring them back," Andre continued, "I want you to forget about your parents."

Marie stared at Andre, dumbstruck.

"You're always going on about them," Andre said to the water. "I don't know if you noticed, but it makes Mama Boudreau awful sad. She loves you powerful much."

"I know," said Marie. "I don't mean to."

"Then you promise?" asked Andre. "No matter what happens?"

Marie nodded.

"Nodding's not nothin'," said Andre. "You got to say it."

"I promise," whispered Marie.

"Good," said Andre, helping her to her feet. "I'll walk you in. It's getting late."

Marie thought hard about the shoes and the promise all night long. She was listening so hard for angels that she missed when Mama Boudreau asked her to pass the lima beans at dinner. She was looking so closely for ghosts in the corners that she tripped going up the stairs to bed. She lay under the covers listening to the wind at the window, the shoes poking straight up at the end of the bedsheets. Marie prayed with all her might before she fell asleep. This was her last chance.

Her dreams were empty. The only part of them she could remember was staring down at a black baby doll in a rusty crib, its eyes and teeth made out of cotton stuffing.

She cried when she woke, hiding her sobs in the pillow so Mama Boudreau wouldn't hear.

True to her word, Marie slowly and painfully made her way back to Voodoo Lily's antique shop. When she got there, there was a woman in a pale cotton dress sitting on the stoop. Her red gold hair fell past her shoulders. She had a bag of popcorn in her lap and was gobbling it up by the handful. "Shop's closed," she mumbled.

"I came to give Voo—Miss Lily her shoes back," Marie said to the woman. She started to slide her feet out of them.

"Wait!" screeched the woman. "Did they work?"

"No," Marie said sadly. "They didn't."

The woman stood up. She was very tall. She rolled her popcorn bag closed and rested it on the empty stoop. She held a hand out to Lily. "It's not raining yet."

Marie took the woman's hand. It was cool and soft. Together they walked to the end of the street. Marie imagined they made quite a pair — a small girl shuffling in her too-big shoes beside a tall woman in worn, green flip-flops who kind of walked like a duck.

The street ended at the edge of the bayou. Marie could see across the low water to Devil's Island and the tall tree in the middle of it.

"Did you try going there?" asked the woman.

Marie furrowed her brow. "I can't make it out there," she said.

"I'd have to swim. The shoes would come off."

The woman smiled down at her. "You have to believe," she said.

Marie was so sad, so tired, so beaten that she didn't bother to question the woman. She slid down the bank of the bayou and held one shoe-clad foot out over the murky water. She sighed and dropped her leg.

There was no splash, no wet, no squish of mud around her toes. The shoe remained perfectly dry, resting on top of the water like it was hard land. Marie looked back at the woman in shock. The woman waved her on.

Step by magic step, Marie walked across the bayou to Devil's Island. When the shoes touched muddy land, the tree disappeared. In its place was a small gazebo surrounded by green grass and a rainbow of multicolored irises.

A woman and a man sat inside the gazebo, shaded from the heat of the morning sun. The woman had short hair and a pert nose. Her little hands worked at knitting needles that flew so fast, Marie could barely follow them. The man leaned back against a post, his hands folded over his chest. His eyes were closed.

"Hello?" Marie asked, but neither seemed to be able to hear her.

"Do you think she wonders about us, Robert?" the woman asked.

"Who, Nina?"

"Our daughter," said Nina.

Robert opened his eyes. "Marie," he said. "They called her Marie."

Nina nodded. "It's a good name." She set her needles down in her lap. "I think about her all the time. I feel bad."

Marie gasped. These people were talking about *her*! "Mama?" she asked tentatively. "Papa?"

"I know," said Robert, oblivious to Marie's questions.

"It's just…you were so sick," said Nina. "I couldn't leave you. And then I got sick…"

Robert put an arm around his wife. "You did what you had to," he told her. "She found a good home. She's grown into a beautiful girl. And one day, she'll understand."

Nina looked up at him. "She'll know that we loved her?"

Robert kissed her on the forehead. "She'll know."

"I know," whispered Marie. "I know!" She wanted to run to them, make them see her, but her feet seemed rooted to the ground. "Mama!" she cried. "Papa!"

A cool hand touched her arm. "They can't hear you," said the woman.

Marie wrapped her arms around the woman and sobbed into her shoulder. The woman patted her hair and rubbed her back until Marie pulled away. She sniffed and hiccupped, wiping the tears from her eyes.

"Are you ready to go?" the woman asked.

Marie took a long last look at the figures in the gazebo. She tried to burn into her memory every nuance of their features, but she knew she didn't have to. She would see them both every time she looked in the mirror. She turned back to the woman and nodded.

"Just take off the shoes," the woman said.

Marie started to slide her left foot out and then paused. She cocked her head and looked at the woman, at the morning sun glinting off her red-gold hair. "Can *you* talk to them?"

"No," the woman smiled. "They's dead folk. I only talk to angels."

***

Marie stood alone and barefoot on the stoop of the dark antique shop, the giant wooden shoes lying silently three inches in front of her big toes. Her heart felt light and hurt all at the same time.

She could keep her promise. To everyone.

Water trickled down her legs and pooled around her toes.

She closed her eyes and smiled up into the rain.

THE WERE FOUR

"I told you he was going to freak out," said Quinn.

"Quick! Grab him!" said Peter.

"No way, man. I'm not going anywhere near those teeth," said Sam.

"You pissed him off, Peter," said Quinn. "You save him."

"*You* made the joke," said Peter.

"*You* renamed the band," said Sam.

"You are both pussies," said Peter, and he ran to get his mom's heavy-duty gloves from the kitchen.

"Who's talking, fuzzy ass?" Sam yelled up the stairs after him.

Peter dove into the cupboard under the sink. No gloves. What the hell? Didn't all moms keep gloves under the sink? Peter growled his frustration.

"What's up?" asked Natalie. Sam's little sister was perched on the counter eating Girl Scout cookies and reading a *Gothic Beauty* magazine.

"Get your giant stompin' boots off the counter, Natalie."

"Shut up your mother loves me." It was mostly annoying because it was true. "What's going on?"

"Romeo flipped."

"Aw, jeez." Natalie leapt off the counter. It was an impressive move, as the knee-high platform leather boots she had gotten for Christmas must have weighed a third of her body mass. She threw open the door to the basement, spread her arms to grab a railing with each hand, and slid down the stairs, which annoyed Peter even further. He still couldn't do that, even without shoes.

By the time Peter reached the bottom of the stairs, Natalie had taken off her hoodie and tossed it over Romeo's flipping, snapping body. She quickly scooped the bundle up in her arms.

"Where's the tank?" she asked.

"It busted a couple of months ago," said Sam.

"'Cause Sam tried to use it as an amp stand," said Quinn.

"We haven't gotten it fixed," said Peter. "Romeo's been fairly calm lately."

The bundle thrashed wildly in her arms. "Toilet then."

Quinn ran ahead and opened the door to the bathroom for her. Peter thought Romeo might have preferred the sink, but before he could even suggest it, Natalie flipped her hoodie inside out and Romeo splashed into the toilet. It took him a moment to recover, but he quickly started swimming angry circles around the bowl.

Natalie dropped the hoodie and put her hands on her skinny hips. "What did you say to him?"

Peter stared at Sam, but Quinn and Sam stared back at him harder. He sighed in defeat. "I signed us up for the Annapolis Battle of the Bands because we forgot to do it before 'cause we weren't sure we were even going to do it at all 'cause we only have like three songs but I signed up just in case 'cause we can always change our minds whenever and the deadline was today but when I did I changed the name of the band," he said in one breath.

"Good," said Natalie. "'Maelstrom' was kind of stupid." She preemptively crossed her eyes and stuck her tongue out at Quinn and Sam.

"I forgot how to spell it," said Peter.

"Sam kept calling us 'Male Storm' anyway," said Quinn.

"So now we're The Were Four," said Peter.

Natalie snorted. "Okay."

"And then nerd-ass here had to go and quote Shakespeare." Peter punched Sam on the shoulder for good measure.

Natalie groaned. She scrunched up her nose and said, "Were-four art thou, Romeo." Quinn did a spit take and laughed so hard he doubled over. Sam smiled that famous shit-eating grin of his. Okay, fine. Peter had to admit it was kind of funny. He remembered Romeo's reaction and snickered a little himself. The piranha in the toilet jumped and snapped at them.

"Dude," Natalie said to the fish. "They're *your* friends."

"He is going to be so pissed when he calms down," said Sam. Quinn was still laughing to hard to comment.

"Just remember not to flush him," said Natalie.

"Finding Romeo!" said Sam. "Quick! Call Pixar!"

"Oh, god," said Peter.

Quinn guffawed and wiped tears away. "Holy crap," he said, gasping for breath, "I'm gonna pee my pants."

"Just as long as you don't use the toilet," said Natalie. "I'm going to get his clothes. Here"—she threw her hoodie at Peter—"I'd rather not smell like fish."

"Romeo wouldn't mind if you did," said Quinn.

Sam punched Quinn, who gave up at that point and fell over.

"Don't talk about my sister."

"Just talk about his mama," said Peter. Sam slapped him in the back of the head. Peter tripped over Quinn, still laughing in a fetal position, and they all went sprawling on the floor.

"Excuse me." Natalie gave Sam a courtesy kick in the ass with a giant boot as she stepped over them. She folded the clothes neatly and set them beside the sink. Peter managed to get Sam in a headlock. Quinn yanked the hoodie out of Peter's hands and whipped it around his head. The room went dark and smelled like Dad's tackle box right before Quinn and Sam sat on him.

"I ha-ave to pe-ee!" laughed Quinn.

"Get the hell off me, douche!" yelled Peter.

He heard Natalie shut the bathroom door, and then the clomp of her boots before the basement lights blinded them again. "Give me this. Morons."

Once Quinn ran upstairs to pee, it was easy enough for Peter to shove Sam's puny ass onto the floor. He hopped onto the dryer and watched Natalie shake the Tide bottle. "You got any more of this?" Peter shrugged. "Fine. I'll just try to rinse out what's in here." She pulled the knob on the machine and filled the empty bottle with water, then dumped out the suds.

"I suppose we could have put Romeo in the washing machine," said Peter.

"I'm sure it wouldn't be the first time," she said.

"So what do you think of our new name?" he asked.

She shrugged. "It's fine." She threw her hoodie in the washer and closed the lid. "When's this Battle of the Bands thing?"

"This weekend."

She raised an eyebrow. "Aren't you grounded this weekend?"

"Technically."

"*Technically?*"

"Well, I sort of have a way around that."

"Really."

"And I sort of need your help."

Natalie raised both eyebrows this time.

"*We* need your help."

"So what's the prize for this Battle of the Bands?"

Thinking about the prize energized Peter all over again. "The winner gets to open for Stephen Kellogg and the Sixers when they play Annapolis."

"Stephen Who? Never heard of them."

"It's four guys—they're influenced by Tom Petty and Pearl Jam and their lyrics are a-ma-zing."

"You guys don't sound like Tom Petty *or* Pearl Jam," said Natalie. "And if I had a dollar for every time you rhymed 'death' with 'breath,' these Sixers would be opening up for *me*."

"Stephen Kellogg's motto is 'Dare to Suck,'" said Sam.

"He should have dared you to practice more," said Natalie.

"We're gonna go and we're gonna be *awesome*," said Peter, because it was true.

"The second thing's a matter of a opinion," said Natalie. "As for the first…good luck with that."

"That's where we need your help," said Peter.

"She's going to say no," said Sam.

"As much as I hate to agree with my brother, he's right," said Natalie.

"Come on, Natalie. You don't even know what I'm going to ask you yet."

"I know that I've never once been invited to join your little boys-only club, unless it's to make brownies or rescue Romeo," she said.

"You do make good brownies," said Sam.

"You've never let me practice with you," said Natalie. "And I play drums better than Sam."

"My dog plays drums better than Sam," said Quinn. He skipped down the last two steps and vaulted the back of the ratty green couch.

"Hear me out," said Peter. "I have a plan."

Natalie sat down next to Quinn. The ten rows of buckles on her ginormous boots scraped by each other as she crossed her legs. "This not only better be good, but it also better include some serious financial gain on my part."

"We could let you play with us sometime?" Peter said hesitantly.

"Or NOT," Quinn and Sam said in unison.

At a splash, thump, and growl, everyone turned to the bathroom door. After a few minutes Romeo emerged, redressed in ripped jeans and vintage TRON t-shirt. His dark skin still glistened with damp, and what short black hair he had stuck up in crazy spikes. "The toilet? Really?" The words echoed in his barrel chest. Not for the first time, Peter wished he had filled out a little more in his junior year. Romeo was built like a Polynesian linebacker and could easily eat the rest of his band mates for breakfast. Natalie, whose lanky height combined with her boots made her the only one who could see eye to eye with Romeo, attacked him in a flying leap. Romeo caught the hug and swung her around. "Hey, little sista."

"Romeo! I'm sorry I put you in the toilet. Those idiots gave me no choice. I was afraid you were going to die."

"We were afraid you were going to bite us," said Quinn.

"I still might," said Romeo. He pointed at Sam. "Except for him. Him I'm gonna kill."

"Can I watch?" asked Natalie.

"You know you love me," said Sam, with less confidence than he probably meant.

"I'd love to put my hands around your scrawny neck," said Romeo. "But I will restrain myself out of respect for your sister."

"Aw," said Natalie.

Romeo shot Quinn a look and he quickly vacated the couch so that Romeo could sit. Natalie cuddled up to him. Platonic brotherliness aside, Peter suspected the reason Natalie really loved Romeo so much was because he was the only one of them who had the ability to make Natalie look small. "So," he said. "Where were we before stupid got the better of me?"

"Natalie was just agreeing to drive us to the Battle of the Bands on Friday," said Peter.

"I did what?" asked Natalie.

"She did what?" asked Sam.

"Sweet," said Quinn.

"You know I only have a learner's permit." Natalie narrowed her eyes at Peter. "And Friday is the full moon."

"That's what makes this perfect!" His plan really was perfect.

"Nobody's ever out on the roads during a full moon." It was true. In 2012, the world hadn't ended, but life as they'd known it did. Without warning, some crazy celestial event timed with that damned Mayan calendar turned ninety-nine percent of the world's population into their totem animal. Cities now ground to a halt during the full moon. Sure, some weres still did the Jekyll and Hyde thing, like Romeo, or the physical exhaustion thing, like Sam, but that one inevitable night every month, every human on the planet was considerably indisposed. Every human, that is, except the less-than-one percentage of the population who were Unwere. Like Natalie.

"Jerk," said Natalie. For some reason, she still didn't like anyone bringing her normalcy to attention. Peter didn't understand why. It's not like he looked forward to sitting around for an entire night watching *Phineas and Ferb* and scratching his stupidly furry butt with his stupidly long beak. It wasn't like he'd matured enough to have venomous spurs on his hind feet, and even if he had, it's not like he planned on doing anything with them. While he was a platypus, he was only ever concerned with where his next worm or shrimp was coming from or if the webbing between his toes was drying out.

The way Peter figured, it was better to be *no* were than a *lame* were. All the athletic guys at his school were wolves and bears and elephants. All the hot chicks were ponies and swans and cats. He looked at his friends: sloth, mosquito, piranha. Sure, Romeo was dangerous, but how dangerous was a single piranha, really? Romeo had ditched his buff sham friends after the third time he came within an inch of death at a frat party. It was like the Celestial Event cemented them all in their current status and doomed them to never be cool. Ever.

Natalie could do *whatever she wanted*. It was like being the only person in the world on a regular, temporary basis. Oh, the things he would do... For some reason, all Natalie did was break up with all her very old and very popular friends, dress in black, and dye her hair rainbow colors. She always had her nose stuck in some book or another; she didn't really talk to anybody anymore. In fact, Peter realized, he'd spoken to Natalie more in the last ten minutes than he had in the last five months.

"Just hear me out," he told her. "Wait until everybody's in wereform, then just shove us all in Romeo's van and drive to Annapolis. It's only like an hour and a half away, and there will be *no traffic*. Who gets no traffic in D.C.? Like, ever?"

"I'll have to spend the night somewhere. I am not sleeping in the van with you and Sam's drum kit."

"We'll get you a hotel room," said Romeo. When the others balked, Romeo repeated, "*We'll get you a hotel room*," just in case he hadn't gotten his point across.

"I'll leave Mom a note that I'm staying over at your place," said Peter.

"But you're grounded," said Natalie. "Am I the only one who remembers this? You and Quinn tried to walk to Walmart that one night, and the cop picked you up with four cans of spray paint?"

"Yeeeeah," said Peter. "Well, she hasn't said anything. I don't plan on bringing it up. And if she does remember, it'll be too late. I'm gonna have to play forgiveness versus permission on this one."

"This is really worth that much to you?" she asked.

"Yes," said Peter. More than chocolate and Cheetos and peanut butter sandwiches. He made his most pitiful, depressed kicked-puppy face.

Natalie rolled her eyes. "Fine."

Sam, Quinn, and Peter attempted a three-way high-five and failed miserably. Romeo shook his head and rummaged in his pocket for his keys. "Come on," he said to Natalie. "Let's take the van around the block a couple of times so you can get a feel for it. These yahoos need to practice."

"Perfect," said Natalie. "Outside the house is the best place to be for that anyway."

***

Peter woke naked and shivering in the back of Romeo's van. He stretched his limbs and splayed his no-longer-webbed fingers wide apart. He shifted to pull the drumstick out from under his lower back and took a few deep breaths as his eyes slowly adjusted back to human. Romeo had already de-wered and left the van. Peter didn't blame him. Sam still laid there, a blanket bunched beneath his still body with its long limbs, flat face, and tiny ears. Peter didn't have a blanket. He shivered again. Doubtless that was part of Natalie's subtle revenge. He ruffled Sam's backward fur and decided that sloth-Sam didn't look all that different from human-Sam.

He couldn't tell if Quinn had changed back or not; he certainly didn't see a mosquito or hear one buzzing about, but who ever did until it was too late? Peter pushed himself into a sitting position and felt a bundle of clothes under his hand. His clothes. Maybe Natalie wasn't so mad at his after all. There was another bundle by Sam, but no other. Quinn was up and about then. Good.

As he pulled his jeans on, his phone fell out of his pocket. "Ten o'clock? Already?? Shit!" They had to be set up and ready to perform their first song at noon. "Sam." Peter shook the sloth's body. "Sam!"

The back door of the van opened to reveal Romeo and Natalie, standing in a parking lot Peter had never seen before. Annapolis. He smiled—part of him had been worried that Natalie would kidnap them all and then just leave the van parked in the driveway. But his relief was short lived.

"Good morning, Sunshine," said Romeo.

Natalie's greeting was slightly less amiable. "Which of you morons gave Sam energy drinks last night?"

Peter winced. "Quinn brought a six-pack of them. We had to practice as late as we could. I didn't know Sam had any."

"What do you think?" Natalie pointed to the sloth. Sam was kind of hyper ADHD anyway, but when he got worked up, he crashed hard. Too much caffeine or too little sleep, and Sam could be a sloth for days afterward.

Quinn squeezed in beside Natalie and pulled out a blue milk crate of supplies. "He'll wake up. He's just being an asshole and making us unload everything."

"Yeah. Probably," said Peter, passing Natalie a snare drum.

"You better hope so," said Natalie.

"I'll go download a drum machine app on my phone," said Romeo.

"We'll get this all set up and ready, and Sam will wake up just in time to walk on stage," Quinn predicted. "Bastard."

But Sam did not wake up. He didn't wake up when Natalie, acting as the band manager—with some choice words to say about improving her taste in bands—signed them onto the BotB roster. Sam didn't wake up when the guy from the radio station warmed up the smallish crowd in the freezing warehouse. Sam didn't wake up when the first band played their song, nor did he wake up when Peter, Quinn, and Romeo changed into their costumes.

"You look like you've got a job interview," Natalie said of their suits and ties. "Did you find an app?" she asked Romeo.

"I found EZ Beats and a couple others, but they take off points for using them," he told her.

"Every point counts," Quinn reminded her.

"We need all the points we can get," said Romeo.

"Hey, Natalie. You know our songs, right?" Peter asked. He held Sam's bundle of clothes in his arms.

"I hate you." Natalie snatched the bundle of clothes from him. "My giant ass is probably not going to fit in Sam's pants, you know."

"So don't wear the pants," said Peter. "It'll be fine."

"Bathroom's over there," said Romeo.

"We go on in three songs," said Romeo.

Natalie was already walking away. "I'll be there," she said, "but I'll still hate you."

"I'm gonna kill Sam," Peter said to his bandmates.

"I was already planning on killing Quinn," said Romeo.

"Let's just tune up the guitars and stuff, okay?" Quinn asked, hurrying over to their gear in an attempt to avoid death.

"I left Sam in the parking lot," Romeo said, "with blankets and clothes and a note saying where we are. It's cold, but I figured it would be better than him waking up in a strange hotel room somewhere."

"You're probably right. Good thinking," said Peter. "Man, if he misses all this, he'll be pissed."

"If he misses all this, I'll be pissed," said Quinn.

"Natalie might be able to pull it off," said Romeo. Peter and Quinn paused long enough to give him a what-the-hell-is-wrong-with-you-and-the-planet-you-fell-from look. Romeo shrugged it off. "I'm just sayin'."

"The only thing Natalie's good at is stomping around in those boots," said Peter.

"And she's not even great at that," said Quinn.

"I'm not great at what?" asked Natalie.

Peter was on his knees plugging in a pedal when the boots in question stomp onto the stage. He looked up at Natalie, and up, and up. She was wearing Sam's collared shirt and tie, and those damned boots. And nothing else.

"Woah, girl," said Romeo.

Peter cursed. "Sam's gonna kill me," he said.

Quinn turned red and looked away.

"I told you the pants wouldn't fit," she said innocently.

Peter snapped. "I said don't wear *his* pants. Not don't wear *any* pants!"

Natalie bent her long arms and put her hands on her hips the way she always did. Not that Peter could be sure they were her hips, since he was fairly certain her legs just went all the way up to her armpits.

At the first catcall, he realized they were drawing a crowd. *All* the crowd. He peered around Natalie to where the assembly could probably see her underwear. If she was wearing underwear. Oh, god, they were all going to go to jail.

"Let the girl play!" screamed an audience member.

"Let her do whatever she wants," shouted another.

Romeo caught Natalie up in a bear hug and physically moved her to the seat behind Sam's drum set. Had Peter thought Sam's bass drum was huge before? It clearly still wasn't big enough. He could still see Natalie's white knees peeking out from behind it above those damn boots.

"Play!" yelled an audience member.

"We're not up yet," Peter yelled back. He pulled his guitar strap up over his shoulder.

"You are now," said the guy from the radio station. He leapt on to the stage with them. "We'll shuffle people if we have to. All I know is that this poor crowd is freezing their asses off, and they need something to get excited about. Are you guys ready to rock?" He said the last part into his microphone.

Peter strummed a chord in answer.

"Ladies and Gentlemen, I give you The Were Four!"

The crowd went wild.

It was the only time the whole night the crowd went wild. Unfortunately, all that enthusiasm didn't make The Were Four suck any less. The pace was too fast, the monitors stank, and the guys constantly yelling at Natalie to take her clothes off distracted Quinn and Peter, who suddenly couldn't seem to remember which verses cam before the chorus. To make matter worse, every time he sang the words 'death' and 'breath' he tried not to cringe.

It was horrible. By the time they got voted out of the third round, it didn't exactly hurt anyone's feelings. They only had three original songs anyway.

Romeo and Quinn gave Peter a consoling pat on the back, but it didn't matter. Peter was still elated. He still remembered the way the crowd had gone crazy in anticipation. He wouldn't be opening for the Sixers now—or any time soon—but he had that feeling. One day, he'd feel it again. He bent down to unplug his guitar and saw boots. He tried not to look at anything else as he stood up.

"You must be freezing," he said.

As always, she ignored him. "I'm sorry we didn't win."

Peter shrugged, but he was still smiling. "It's okay. We sucked."

"Hey, at least we dared to," said Natalie.

"Yeah," said Peter. "We did."

Natalie flipped the drumsticks around in her fingers. "Do you think I can play with you guys again sometime?"

"Maybe."

"You'll have to change the name of the band, though," she said.

"Oh, right. What about 'The Not-Entirely-Were Four?"

"How about 'Natalie and the Were Four?"

Peter laughed. "I'm gonna have to think about that one."

"You do that," she said, and then she kissed him. On the lips. Not a box-office sizzler, but not a sisterly kiss either. "Thanks," she said.

Peter didn't say anything. He didn't know what to say. He just watched those very tall boots and those very long legs walk away. He felt a tap on his shoulder and turned around long enough to get punched in the face.

Sam was awake.

ACKNOWLEDGEMENTS

Thanks to my dearest sister-scribe J.T. Ellison, for suggesting this collection in the first place.

Thanks to my bosom companion Leanna, for being a beautiful soul cut from my same magical cloth. I'm so happy we found each other!

Thanks to Adam Ezra and the entire Adam Ezra group, for writing songs that continue to inspire me, and having performances that make me want to dance my face off.

Thanks to Steven Saus, for helping me put it all together the first time around.

Thanks to Luc Reid, James Maxey, Eric James Stone, and the rest of the Codex Writers Group, without whom many of these stories would not have been written.

Thanks to the amazingly talented supernova that is Kate Baker, for performing an audiobook the likes of which I never dreamed I'd have.

Thanks *again* to Jason Anderson for another fine layout and Rachel Marks for one more gorgeous book cover, the kind that dreams are made of.

And thanks to all of you, my friends, who remember that a princess can dwell in darkness sometimes…and aren't afraid to join me there.

About the Author

New York Times and USA Today bestselling author Alethea Kontis is a princess, a fairy godmother, and a geek. She's known for screwing up the alphabet, scolding vampire hunters, and ranting about fairy tales on YouTube.

Alethea's published works include: *The Wonderland Alphabet* (with Janet K. Lee), *Diary of a Mad Scientist Garden Gnome* (with Janet K. Lee), the AlphaOops series (with Bob Kolar), the Books of Arilland fairy tale series, and *The Dark-Hunter Companion* (with Sherrilyn Kenyon). Her short fiction, essays, and poetry have appeared in a myriad of anthologies and magazines.

Her YA fairy tale novel, *Enchanted*, won both the Gelett Burgess Children's Book Award and Garden State Teen Book Award. *Enchanted* was nominated for the Audie Award in 2013 and was selected for World Book Night in 2014. Both *Enchanted* and its sequel, *Hero*, were nominated for the Andre Norton Award. *Tales of Arilland*, a short story collection set in the same fairy tale world, won a second Gelett Burgess Award in 2015.

Princess Alethea was given the honor of speaking about fairy tales at the Library of Congress in 2013. In 2015, she gave a keynote address at the Lewis Carroll Society's Alice150 Conference in New York City, celebrating the 150th anniversary of *Alice's Adventures in Wonderland*. She also enjoys speaking at schools and festivals all over the US. (If forced to choose between all these things, she says middle schools are her favorite!)

Born in Burlington, Vermont, Alethea currently lives and writes on the Space Coast of Florida. She makes the best baklava you've ever tasted and sleeps with a teddy bear named Charlie. You can find Princess Alethea on her YouTube channel, all the social media, and at her website: www.aletheakontis.com.